The Vanishing of Betty Varian

By Carolyn Wells

Originally published in 1923

The Vanishing of Betty Varian

© 2011 Resurrected Press
www.ResurrectedPress.com

Published by Resurrected Press

This classic book was handcrafted by Resurrected Press. Resurrected Press is dedicated to bringing high quality classic books back to the readers who enjoy them. These are not scanned versions of the originals, but, rather, quality checked and edited books meant to be enjoyed!

Please visit ResurrectedPress.com to view our entire catalogue!

ISBN 13: 978-1-937022-24-2

Printed in the United States of America

FOREWORD

The mysteries of Carolyn Wells are unlike those of most of her contemporaries. Wells had originally been a successful writer of humorous verse until she turned her had to detective fiction after reading a novel of Anna Katherine Green. While the fashion in mysteries of the time was centered on puzzles and elaborate clues and the cleverness of the detective in deciphering them, Wells was much more concerned with the people affected by the crime and their interactions with each other both before and after the events.

She wrote mainly about the class of people she herself was a part of—the upper middle class of the east coast, particularly New York and the adjacent areas of New Jersey. Her characters are doctors, lawyers, and businessmen and their wives, daughters, and lovers. Writing at a time when women were still largely subservient to men, she often invoked the tensions of the various domestic relationships, whether it is that between a husband and a wife or between a father and his daughter. These tensions serve as motives that cause suspicion to fall, whether correctly or not, on the characters in the story.

Some critics have suggested that Wells' mysteries are often contrived. It is certainly true that she was perhaps overly fond of various architectural trickeries such as secret passages and hidden doors. But these were regular features of detective fiction of the era, and those that appear in Wells' work are neither more or less believable than most. However, they are never the central part of the story as they so often are with her contemporaries. Rather, it is the social and psychological aspects that are of primary interest.

The Vanishing of Betty Varian is one of Wells' darker mysteries. Of course, most of her works involve a murder, but in *Betty Varian* several possibilities for the crimes are presented, both of which would evoke horror in her readers. In one case, the daughter has murdered her father. In the another, the daughter has been murdered by the father who then commits suicide. And in yet a third, the daughter is a victim of a kidnapping and the father was murdered while trying to prevent it. It is not until well into the book that which is the correct possibility becomes clear. Meanwhile, the characters are casting recriminations and aspersions on both the living and dead. It is the psychology and not the detection that makes Wells' work so interesting.

One of the biggest mysteries of the all the Pennington Wise novels is the young woman known only as Zizi. The exact nature of her relationship with the detective is never spelled out. Confusingly, she is portrayed as both a child and young woman, her occupation variously as an artist's model and an occasional film actress, and described as a witch or gypsy. It is hard to believe that Pennington Wise, a bachelor in his thirties, could travel openly with a female minor, though it would be little more acceptable at the time if she was of age. Certainly, the way in which she addresses Wise is not that of a dependent, though there is never a hint of romance in the novels. At its best, the banter between the two of them presages that of the "screwball comedies" of the 1930's. Zizi, then, must be looked on as an early example of a "liberated" woman and perhaps a bit of wishful thinking on the part of Wells.

The works of Carolyn Wells are not as well known today as they were when she was writing them. This is unfortunate, as they give the modern reader a glimpse of an era that is now past, while maintaining an intrinsic interest on their own. It is therefore with pleasure that Resurrected Press is pleased to offer this edition of *The Vanishing of Betty Varian*.

About the Author

Carolyn Wells, June 18, 1862 - March 26, 1942 was an American writer and poet. She was best known for her books of poetry and humor until around 1910 she read one of Anna Katherine Green's mysteries and took up the genre. Many of her mysteries featured the detective Fleming Stone. She was married to Hadwin Houghton, heir to the Houghton-Mifflin publishing company. She was a collector of poetry by other authors, and, upon her death, she bequeathed her collection of the works of Walt Witman to the Library of Congress.

Greg Fowlkes
Editor-In-Chief
Resurrected Press
www.ResurrectedPress.com

Table of Contents

CHAPTER 1: HEADLAND HARBOR

IT is, of course, possible, perhaps even probable, that somewhere on this green earth there may be finer golf links or a more attractive clubhouse than those at Headland Harbor, but never hope to wring such an admission from any one of the summer colony who spend their mid-year at that particular portion of the Maine coast.

Far up above the York cliffs are more great crags and among the steepest and wildest of these localities, a few venturesome spirits saw fit to pitch their tents.

Others joined them from time to time until now, the summer population occupied nearly a hundred cottages and bungalows and there was, moreover, a fair sized and fairly appointed inn.

Many of the regulars were artists, of one sort or another, but also came the less talented in search of good fishing or merely good idling. And they found it, for the majority of the householders were people of brains as well as talent and by some mysterious management the tone of the social side of things was kept pretty much as it should be.

Wealth counted for what it was worth, and no more. Genius counted in the same way, and was never overrated. Good nature and an amusing personality were perhaps the best assets one could bring to the conservative little community, and most of the shining lights possessed those in abundance.

To many, the word harbor connotes a peaceful, serene bit of blue water, sheltered from rough winds and basking in the sunlight.

This is far from a description of Headland Harbor, whose rocky shores and deep black waters were usually wind-swept and often storm-swept to a wild picturesqueness beloved of the picture painters.

But there were some midsummer days, as now, one in late July, when the harbor waters lay serene and the sunlight dipped and danced on the tiny wavelets that broke into spray over the nearby rocks.

Because it was about the hour of noon, the clubhouse verandah was crowded with members and guests waiting for the mail, which, as always, was late.

The clubhouse, a big, low building, with lots of shiny paint and weathering shingles, was at the nearest spot consistent with safety to the shore. From it could be had a magnificent view of the great headland that named the place.

This gigantic cliff jutted out into the sea, and rising to a height of three hundred feet, the mighty crag showed a slight overhang which rendered it unscalable. The wet black rock glistened in the sunlight, as spray from the dashing breakers broke half way up its sides.

The top was a long and narrow tableland, not much more than large enough to accommodate the house that crowned the summit. There was a strip of sparse lawn on either side the old mansion, and a futile attempt at a garden, but vegetation was mostly confined to the weird, one-sided pine trees that waved the branches of their lee sides in mournful, eerie motions.

"Can't see how any one wants to live up there in that God-forsaken shack," said John Clark, settling more comfortably in his porch rocker and lighting a fresh cigarette.

"Oh, I think it's great!" Mrs. Blackwood disagreed with him. "So picturesque—"

"You know, if you say 'picturesque' up here, you'll be excommunicated. The thing is all right, but the word is taboo."

"All right, then, chromoesque."

"But it isn't that," Clark objected; "it's more like an old steel engraving—"

"Oh, not with all that color," said Lawrence North. "It is like an engraving on a gray, cloudy day,—but today, with the bright water and vivid sunshine, it's like a—"

"Speak it right out!" cried Ted Landon, irrepressibly, "like a picture postcard!"

"It can't help being like that," Mrs. Blackwood agreed, "for the postcards for sale in the office of the club are more like the reality than any picture an artist has ever made of the Headland House."

"Of course, photographs are truer than drawings," North said, "and that card that shows the cliff in a storm comes pretty near being a work of art."

"The difficulty would be," Clark observed, "to get any kind of a picture of that place that wouldn't be a work of art. Why, the architect's blueprints of that house would come a good deal nearer art than lots of watercolors I've seen in exhibitions. I'm keen on the place."

"Who isn't?" growled Landon, for most of the Headlanders resented the faintest disparagement of their cherished masterpiece, a joint work of nature and man.

The promontory was joined to the mainland by a mere narrow neck of rocky land, and from that point a rough road descended, over and between steep hills, reaching at last the tiny village and scattered settlement of Headland Harbor.

Headland House itself was a modified type of old world architecture. Built of rough gray stone, equipped with a few towers and turrets, pierced by deep and narrow windows, it had some effects of a French chateau and others that suggested an old English castle.

It was true to no school, it followed no definite type, yet perched on its lonely height, sharply outlined against the sky, its majestic rock foundations sweeping away from beneath it, it showed the grandeur and sublimity of a well-planned monument.

And, partly because of their real admiration, partly because of a spirit of ownership, the artist colony loved and cherished their Headland House with a jealous sensitiveness to criticism.

"Stunning thing,—from here," John Clark said, after a few moments of further smoking and gazing; "all the same, as I stated, I shouldn't care to live up there."

"Too difficult of access," Claire Blackwood said, "but, otherwise all right."

Mrs Blackwood was a widow, young, attractive, and of a psychic turn of mind. Not enough of an occultist to make her a bore, but possessing quick and sure intuitions and claiming some slight clairvoyant powers. She dabbled in water colors, and did an occasional oil. She was long-limbed, with long fingers and long feet, and usually had a long scarf of some gauzy texture trailing about her. Of an evening or even on a dressy afternoon, she had a long panel or sash-end hanging below her short skirt, and which was frequently trodden on by blundering, inattentive feet.

Good-looking, of course, Claire Blackwood was,—she took care to be that,—but her utmost care could not make her beautiful,—much to her own chagrin. Her scarlet lips were too thin, and the angle of her jaw too hard. Yet she was handsome, belief in her own importance, she was the leader socially, notwithstanding the fact that the colony disclaimed any society element in its life.

"Tell us about the Headland House people, Claire. You've called, haven't you?"

This from Ted Landon, who by reason of his sheer impudence was forgiven any unconventionality. No other man at the Harbor would have dreamed of addressing Mrs. Blackwood by her first name.

"Yes; I've called. They're delightful people." The words said more than the tone.

"With reservations?" asked North.

"Oh, in a way. They're quite all right,—it's only that they're not picture mad,—as we all are."

"Ignorant?"

"Oh, no,—not that. Well, I'll sketch them for you. Mr. Varian is a Wall Street man,—"

"Magnate?"

"Yes, I daresay. Wealthy, anyway. He's big and Vandyke-bearded. Well mannered,—but a bit preoccupied,—if—"

"Yes, we get what you mean," said the irrepressible Ted. "Go on,—what about the daughter?"

"I haven't come to her yet. The mother is due first. Mrs. Varian is the clingingest vine I ever saw. I only saw her on parade, of course, but I'm positive that in curl-papers, she can whine and fret and fly into nervous spasms! Her husband spoils her,—he's far too good to her,—"

"What a lot you gathered at one interview," murmured Lawrence North.

"That's what I went for," Mrs. Blackwood returned, coolly. "Well. Mother Varian is wrapped up in her blossom-child. Betty is a peach,—as I know you boys will agree,—but I never saw greater idolatry in any mother than Mrs. Varian shows."

"Betty worth it?" asked John Clark, idly.

"Rather!" Mrs. Blackwood assured him. "She's a dear thing. I don't often enthuse over young girls, but Betty Varian is unusual."

"As how?"

"Prettier than most girls, more charm, better manners, and,—a suspicion of brains. Not enough to hurt her, but enough to make it a pleasure to talk to her. Moreover, she's a wilful, spoiled, petted darling of two worshipping parents, and it's greatly to her credit that she isn't an arrogant, impossible chit."

"Sounds good to me," commented Ted; "when can I meet her?"

"I'll introduce you soon. They want to meet some of our best people "

"Of course. That lets me in at once. When will you take me?"

"Tomorrow afternoon. They're having a small picnic and they asked me to bring two amusing young men."

"May I go?" asked Lawrence North.

"*Young* men, I said," and Mrs. Blackwood looked at him calmly. "You are old enough to be Betty Varian's father!"

"Well, since I'm not, that needn't prevent my meeting her."

"So you shall, some time. But I'm to take two tomorrow, and,—what do you think? I said I would bring Rodney Granniss, and Mr. Varian said, "No, he'd rather I asked some one in his place!"

"Why, for heaven's sake?" cried Landon. "Rod's our star performer."

"Well, you see, they know him—"

"All the more reason—"

"Oh, it's this way. Rod Granniss is already a beau of Betty's,—and her father doesn't approve of the acquaintance."

"Not approve of Granniss!" John Clark looked his amazement. "Mr. Varian must be an old fuss!"

"I think that's just what he is," assented Claire Blackwood, and then Ted Landon urged, "You haven't described the siren yet. What's she like to look at?"

"A little thing, sylphish, rather,—dainty ways, quick, alert motions, and with the biggest gray eyes you ever saw,—edged with black."

"Raving tresses?"

"No; very dark brown, I think. But the liveliest coloring. Red-under-brown cheeks, scarlet lips and "

"I know,—teeth like pearls."

"No; good, sound, white teeth, and fluttering hands that emphasize and illustrate all she says."

"All right, she'll do," and Ted looked satisfied."I can cut out old John here, and if Granniss isbarred, I'll have a cinch!"

"You must behave yourself,—at first, anyway, because I am responsible for you. Be ready to go up there with me at four tomorrow afternoon."

"Leave here at four?"

"Yes, we'll walk up. A bit of a climb, but motors can go only to the lodge, you know, and that's not worth while."

The porter's lodge belonging to Headland House was partly visible from the clubhouse, and it guarded the gates that gave ingress to the estate. There was no other mode of entrance, for a high wall ran completely across the narrow neck that joined the headland to the main shore, and all other sides of the precipitous cliff ran straight down to the sea.

From where they sat the group could discern the motor road as far as the lodge; and here and there above that could be glimpsed the narrow, tortuous path that led on to the house.

"Grim old pile," Landon said, looking at Headland House. "Any spook connected with its history?"

"I never heard of any," said Mrs. Blackwood.

"Did you, Mr. North?"

"Not definitely, but I've heard vague rumors of old legends or traditions of dark deeds—"

"Oh, pshaw, I don't believe it!" and Mrs. Blackwood shook her head at him. "You're making that up to lend an added interest!"

North grinned. "I'm afraid I was," he admitted, "but if there isn't any legend there surely ought to be. Let's make one up."

"No, I won't have it. I hate haunted houses, and I shan't allow a ghost to be invented. The place is too beautiful to have a foolish, hackneyed old ghost yarn attached to it. Just because you were up here last summer and this is the first year for most of us, you needn't think you can rule the roost!"

"Very well," Lawrence North smiled good-naturedly, "have it your own way. But, truly, I heard rumors last year—"

"Keep them to yourself, then, and when you meet the Varians, as of course you will, don't say anything to them about such a thing."

"Your word is law," and North bowed, submissively. "Here comes the mail at last, and also, here comes Granniss,—the disapproved one!"

A tall outdoorsy-looking young man appeared, and throwing himself into a piazza swing, asked breezily, "Who's disapproving of me, now? Somebody with absolute lack of fine perception!"

"Nobody here," began Landon, and then a warning glance from Claire Blackwood prevented his further disclosures on the subject.

"Don't make a secret of it," went on Granniss, "own up now, who's been knocking poor little me?"

"I," said Mrs. Blackwood, coolly.

"Nixy, Madame Claire! You may disapprove of me, but you're not the one I mean. Who else?"

"Oh, let's tell him," North laughed; "he can stand the shock. They say, Granniss, you're *persona non grata* up at the house on the headland."

Rodney Granniss' eyes darkened and he looked annoyed. But he only said, "That's a disapproval any one may obtain by the simple process of admiring Miss Varian."

"Really?" asked Claire Blackwood.

"Very really. To call twice is to incur the displeasure of one or both parents; to venture a third time is to be crossed out of the guest book entirely."

"But, look here, old man," Landon said, "they've only been in that house about a week. Haven't you been rushing things?"

"I knew them before," said Granniss, simply. "I've met them in New York."

"Oh, well, then their dislike of you is evidently well-founded!"

But this impudence of Landon's brought forth no expression of resentment from its victim. Granniss only winked at Ted, and proceeded to look over his letters.

It was the first time in the memory of any of the present *habitues* of Headland Harbor, that the house on the rocks had been occupied. Built long ago, it was so difficult of access and so high priced of rental that no one had cared to live in it. But, suddenly, and for no known reason, this summer it had been rented, late, and now, toward the end of July, the new tenants were only fairly settled.

That their name was Varian was about all that was known of them, until Mrs. Blackwood's call had been hospitably received and she brought back favorable reports of the family.

It seems Betty was anxious to meet some young people and Mrs. Varian was glad to learn from her caller that small picnics were among the favored modes of entertainment, and she decided to begin that way.

Next day, she explained, a few house guests would arrive, and if Mrs. Blackwood would bring two or three young men and come herself, perhaps that would be enough for a first attempt at sociability.

This met Mrs. Blackwood's entire approval, and she proposed Rodney Granniss' name, all unsuspecting that he would not be welcomed.

"He's all right, you understand," Mrs. Varian had said,—Betty not being then present,—"but he's too fond of my daughter. You can tell,—you know, —and I want the child to have a good time, but I want her to have a lot of young acquaintances, and be friendly with all, but not specially interested in any one. Her father feels the same way,—in fact, he feels more strongly about it even than I do. So, this time, please leave Mr. Granniss out of it."

This was all plausible enough, and no real disparagement to Rodney, so Mrs. Blackwood agreed.

"Can I do anything for you?" she asked her hostess at parting. "Have you everything you want? Are your servants satisfactory?"

"Not in every respect,"—Mrs Varian frowned. "But we're lucky to keep them at all. Only by the most outrageous concessions, I assure you. If they get too overbearing, I may have to let some of them go."

"Let me know, in that case, and I may be able to help you," and with a few further amenities, Claire Blackwood went away.

"But if I were one of her servants I shouldn't stay with her!" she confided later to a trusted friend. "I never saw a more foolishly emotional woman. She almost wept when she told me about her cook's ingratitude! As if any one looked for appreciation of favors in a cook! And when she talked about Betty, she bubbled over with such enthusiasm that she was again moved to tears! It seems her first two little ones died very young, and I think they've always feared they mightn't raise Betty. Hence the spoiling process."

"And it also explains," observed the interested friend, "why the parents discountenance the attentions of would-be swains."

"Of course,—but Betty is twenty, and that is surely old enough to begin to think about such things seriously."

"For the girl,—yes. And doubtless she does. But parents never realize that their infants are growing up. It is not impossible that Rod Granniss and Miss Betty have progressed much further along the road to Arcady than her elders may suspect. Why did the Varians come here,—where Rod is?"

"I don't suppose they knew it,—though, maybe Betty did. Young people are pretty sharp. And you know, Rod was here in June, then he went away and only returned after the Varians arrived. Yes, there must have been some sort of collusion on the part of the youngsters."

"Maybe not. I daresay Miss Betty has lots of admirers as devoted as young Granniss. Can't you ask me to the picnic?"

"Not this one. It's very small. And there are to be some guests at the house, I believe. The family interests me. They are types, I think. Betty is more than an ordinary flutterbudget, like most of the very young girls around here. And the older Varians are really worth while. Mr. Varian is a brooding, self-contained sort,—I feel sorry for him."

"There, there, that will do, Claire! When you feel sorry for a man—I remember you began by being sorry for Lawrence North!"

"I'm sorry for him still. He's a big man,—in a way, a genius,—and yet he—"

"He gets nowhere! That's because he *isn't* a genius! But he's a widower, so he's fair quarry. Don't go to feeling sorry for married men."

"Oh, there's no sentiment in my sympathy for Mr. Varian. Only he intrigues me because of his restless air,—his restrained effect, as if he were using every effort to keep himself from breaking through!"

"Breaking through what?"

"I don't know! Through some barrier, some limit that he has fixed for himself—I tell you I don't know what it's all about. That's why I'm interested."

"Curious, you mean."

"Well, curious, then. And how he puts up with that hand-wringing ready-to-cry wife! Yet, he's fawningly devoted to her! He anticipates her slightest wish,—he is worried sick if she is the least mite incommoded or disturbed,—and I know he'd lie down and let her walk on him if she even looked as if she'd care to!"

"What a lot you read into a man's natural consideration for his wife!"

"But it's there! I'm no fool,—I can read people, —you know that! I tell you that man is under his wife's thumb for some reason far more potent than his love for her, or her demand for affection from him."

"What could be the explanation?"

"I don't know. That's why I'm curious. I'm going to find out, though, and that without the Varians in the least suspecting my efforts. Wait till you see her. She's almost eerie, she's so emotional.

Not noisy or even verbally expressive, but her face is a study in nervous excitement. She seems to grab at the heartstrings of a mere passer-by, and play on them until she tears them out!"

"Good gracious, you make her out a vampire!"

"I think she is,—not a silly vamp, that the girls joke about,—but the real thing!"

CHAPTER 2: BETTY VARIAN

DAD, you're absolutely impossible!"

"Oh, come now, Betty, not as bad as that! Just because I don't agree to everything you say—"

"But you *never* agree with me! You seem to be opposed on principle to everything I suggest or want. It's always been like that! From the time I was born, — how old was I, Dad, when you first saw me?"

Mr Varian looked reminiscent.

"About an hour old, I think," he replied; "maybe a little less."

"Well, from that moment until this, you have persistently taken the opposite side in any discussion we have had."

"But if I hadn't, Betty, there would have been no discussion! And, usually there hasn't been. You're a spoiled baby,—you always have been and always will be. Your will is strong and as it has almost never been thwarted or even curbed, you have grown up a headstrong, wilful, perverse young woman, and I'm sure I don't know what to do with you!"

"Get rid of me, Dad," Betty's laugh rang out, while her looks quite belied the rather terrible character just ascribed to her.

One foot tucked under her, she sat in a veranda swing, now and then touching her toe to the floor to keep swaying. She wore a sand colored sport suit whose matching hat lay beside her on the floor.

Her vivid, laughing face, with its big gray eyes and pink cheeks, its scarlet lips and white teeth was framed by a mop of dark brown wavy hair, now tossed by the strong breeze from the sea.

The veranda overlooked the ocean, and the sunlit waves, stretching far away from the great cliff were dotted in the foreground with small craft.

Frederick Varian sat on the veranda rail, a big, rather splendid looking man, with the early gray of fifty years showing in his hair and carefully trimmed Vandyke beard.

His air was naturally confident and self assured, but in the face of this chit of a girl he somehow found himself at a disadvantage.

"Betty, dear," he took another tack, "can't you understand the fatherly love that cannot bear the idea of parting with a beloved daughter?"

"Oh, yes, but a father's love ought to think what is for that daughter's happiness. Then he ought to make the gigantic self sacrifice that may be necessary."

A dimple came into Betty's cheek, and she smiled roguishly, yet with a canny eye toward the effect she was making.

But Varian looked moodily out over the sea.

"I won't have it," he said, sternly. "I suppose I have some authority in this matter and I forbid you to encourage any young man to the point of a proposal, or even to think of becoming engaged."

"How can I ward off a proposal, Dad?" Betty inquired, with an innocent air.

"Don't be foolish. Of course you can do that. Any girl with your intelligence knows just when an acquaintance crosses the line of mere friendship—"

"Oh, Daddy, you are *too* funny! And when you crossed the line of mere friendship with mother,—what did she do?"

"That has nothing to do with the subject. Now, mind, Betty, I am not jesting,—I am not talking idly—"

"You sound very much like it!"

"I'm not. I'm very much in earnest. You are not to encourage the definite attentions of any—"

"All right, let Rod Granniss come up here then, and I promise not to encourage him."

"He shall not come up here, because he has already gone too far, and you have encouraged him too much—"

"But I love him, Daddy,—and—and I think you might—"

"Hush! That's enough! Don't let me hear another word now or ever regarding Granniss! He is crossed off our acquaintance, and if he persists in staying here, we will go away!"

"Why, Father, we've only just come!"

"I know it, and I came here, thinking to get you away from that man. He followed us up here,—"

"He was here before we came!"

"But he didn't come until he knew we were coming."

"All right, he came because he wanted to be where I am. And I want to be where he is. And you'd better be careful, Father, or I may take the bit in my teeth and—"

"And run off with him? That's why I came here. You can't get away. You perfectly well know that there's no way down from this house but by that one narrow path,— I suppose you've no intention of jumping into the sea?"

"Love will find a way!" Betty sang, saucily.

"It isn't love, Betty. It's a miserable childish infatuation that will pass at once, if you lose sight of the chap for a short time."

"Nothing of the sort! It's the love of my life!"

Varian laughed. "That's a fine sounding phrase, but it doesn't mean anything. Now, child, be reasonable. Give up Granniss. Be friends with all the young people up here, boys and girls both, but don't let me hear any foolishness about being engaged to anybody."

"Do you mean for me never to marry, Father?"

"I'd rather you didn't, my dear. Can't you be content to spend your days with your devoted parents? Think what we've done for you? What we've given you,—"

"Dad, you make me tired! What have you given me, what have you done for me, more than any parents do for a child? You've given me a home, food and clothing,—and loving care! What else? And what do I owe you for that, except my own love and gratitude? But I don't owe you the sacrifice of the natural, normal, expectation of a home and husband of my own! I'm twenty,—that's quite old enough to think of such things. Pray remember how old mother was when she married you. She was nineteen. Suppose her father had talked to her as you're talking to me! What would you have said to him, I'd like to know!"

By this time Fred Varian was walking with quick short strides up and down the veranda. Betty rose and faced him, standing directly in his path.

"Father," she said, speaking seriously, "you are all wrong! You don't know what you're talking about—"

"That will do, Betty!" When Varian's temper was roused he could speak very harshly, and did so now.

"Hush! I will not hear such words from you! How dare you tell me I don't know what I'm talking about! Now you make up your mind to obey me, or I'll cut off all your association with the young people! I'll shut you up—"

"Hush, yourself, Dad! You're talking rubbish, and you know it! Shut me up! In a turret of the castle, I suppose! On bread and water, I suppose! What kind of nonsense is that?"

"You'll see whether it's nonsense or not! What do you suppose I took this isolated place for, except to keep you here if you grow too independent! Do you know there is no way you can escape if I choose to make you a prisoner? And if that's the only way to break your spirit, I'll do it!"

"Why, Father Varian!" Betty looked a little scared, "whatever has come over you?"

"I've made up my mind, that's all. For twenty years I've humored you and indulged you and acceded to your every wish. You've been petted and spoiled until you think you are the only dictator in this family! Now a time has come when I have put my foot down "

"Well, pick it up again, Daddy, and all will be forgiven."

Betty smiled and attempted to kiss the belligerent face looking down at her.

But Frederick Varian repulsed the offered caress and said, sternly:

"I want no affection from a wilful, disobedient child! Give me your word, Betty, to respect my wishes, and I'll always be glad of your loving ways."

But Betty was angry now.

"I'll give you no such promise! I shall conduct myself as I please with my friends and my acquaintances. You know me well enough to know that I never do anything that is in bad form or in bad taste. If I choose to flirt with the young men, or even, as you call it, encourage them, I propose to do so! And I resent your interference, and I deny your right to forbid me in such matters. And, too, I'll go so far as to warn you that if you persist in this queer attitude you've taken,—you'll be sorry! Remember that!"

Betty's eyes flashed, but she was quiet rather than excited.

Varian himself was nervous and agitated. His fingers clenched and his lips trembled with the intensity of his feelings and as Betty voiced her rebellious thoughts he stared at her in amazement.

"What *are* you two quarreling about?" came the surprised accents of Mrs. Varian as she came out through the French window from the library and looked curiously at them.

"Oh, Mother," Betty cried, "Dad's gone nutty! He says I never can marry anybody."

"What nonsense, Fred"; she did not take it at all seriously. "Of course, Betty will marry some day, but not yet. Don't bother about it at present."

"But Daddy's bothering very much about it at present. At least, he's bothering me,—don't let little Betty be bothered, Mummy,—will you?"

"Let her alone, Fred. Why do you tease the child? I declare you two are always at odds over something!"

"No, Minna, that's not so. I always indulge Betty—"

"Oh, yes, after I've coaxed you to do so. You're an unnatural father, Fred, you seem possessed to frown on all Betty's innocent pleasures."

"I don't want her getting married and going off and leaving us—" he growled, still looking angry.

"Well, the baby isn't even engaged yet,—don't begin to worry. And, too, that is in the mother's province.

"Not entirely. I rather guess a father has some authority!"

"Oh, yes, if it's exercised with loving care and discretion. Don't you bother, Betty, anyway. Father and mother will settle this little argument by ourselves."

"I'd rather settle it with Dad," Betty declared spiritedly. "It's too ridiculous for him to take the stand that I shall never marry! I'm willing to promise not to become engaged without asking you both first; I'm willing to say I won't marry a man you can convince me is unworthy; I'm willing to promise anything in reason,—but a blind promise never to marry is too much to ask of any girl!"

"Of course, it is!" agreed Mrs. Varian. "Why do you talk to her like that, Fred?"

"Because I propose to have my own way for once! I've given in to you two in every particular for twenty years or more. Now, I assert myself. I say Betty shall not marry, and I shall see to it that she does not!"

"Oh, my heavens!" and Mrs. Varian wrung her hands, with a wail of nervous pettishness, "sometimes, Fred, I think you're crazy! At any rate, you'll set me crazy, if you talk like that! Do stop this quarrel anyhow. Kiss and make up, won't you? To think of you two, the only human beings on earth that I care a rap for, acting like this! My husband and my child! The only things I live for! The apple of my eye, the core of my soul, both of you,—can't you see how you distress me when you are at odds! And you're always at odds! Always squabbling over some little thing. But, heretofore, you've always laughed and agreed, finally. Now forget this foolishness,—do!"

"It isn't foolishness," and Varian set his lips together, doggedly.

"No, it isn't foolishness," said Betty quietly, but with a look of indomitable determination.

"Well, stop it, at any rate," begged Mrs. Varian, "if you don't I shall go into hysterics,—and it's time now for the Herberts to come."

Now both Fred and Betty knew that a suggestion of hysterics was no idle threat, for Minna Varian could achieve the most annoying demonstrations of that sort at a moment's notice. And it was quite true that the expected guests were imminent.

But no truce was put into words, for just then a party of three people came in sight and neared the veranda steps.

The three were Frederick Varian's brother Herbert and his wife and daughter. This family was called the Herberts to distinguish them from the Frederick Varian household.

The daughter, Eleanor, was a year or two younger than Betty, and the girls were friendly, though of widely differing tastes; the brothers Varian were much alike; but the two matrons were as opposite as it is possible for two women to be. Mrs. Herbert was a strong character, almost strong minded. She had no patience with her sister in law's nerves or hysterical tendencies. It would indeed be awkward if the Herberts were to arrive in the midst of one of Mrs. Frederick's exhibitions of temperamental disturbance.

"Wonderful place!" exclaimed Herbert Varian as they ascended the steps to the verandah. "Great, old boy! I never saw anything like it."

"Reminds me of the Prisoner of Chillon or the Castle of Otranto or—" said Mrs. Herbert.

"Climbing that steep path reminded me of the Solitary Horseman," Herbert interrupted his wife. "Whew! let me sit down! I'm too weighty a person to visit your castled crag of Drachenfels very often! Whew!"

"Poor Uncle Herbert," cooed Betty; "it's an awful long, steep pull, isn't it? Get your breath, and I'll get you some nice, cool fruit punch. Come on, Eleanor, help me; the servants are gone to the circus,—every last one of 'em—"

"Oh, I thought you were having a party here this afternoon," Eleanor said, as she went with Betty.

"Not a party, a picnic. They're the proper caper up here. And only a little one. The baskets are all ready, and the men carry them,—then we go to a lovely picnic place,—not very far,—and we all help get the supper. You see, up here, if you don't let the servants go off skylarking every so often, they leave."

"I should think they would!" exclaimed Eleanor earnestly; "I'm ready to leave now! How do you stand it, Betty? I think it's fearful!"

"Oh, it isn't the sort of thing you'd like, I know. Put those glasses on that tray, will you, Nell? But I love this wild, craggy place, it's like an eagle's eyrie, and I adore the solitude,—especially as there are plenty of people, and a golf club and an artist colony and all sorts of nice things in easy distance."

"You mean that little village or settlement we came through on the way from the station?"

"Yes; and a few of their choicest inhabitants are coming up this afternoon for our picnic."

"That sounds better," Eleanor sighed, "but I'd never want to stay here. Is Rod Grannis here? Is that why you came?"

"Hush, Nell. Don't mention Rod's name, at least, not before Father. You see, Dad's down on him."

"Down on Rod! Why for?"

"Only because he's too fond of little Betty."

"Who is? Rod or your father?"

Betty laughed. "Both of 'em! But, I mean, Dad is down on any young man who's specially interested in me."

"Oh, I know. So is my father. I don't let it bother me. Fathers are all like that. Most of the girls I know say so."

"Yes, I know it's a fatherly failing; but Dad is especially rabid on the subject. There you take the basket of cakes and I'll carry the tray."

It was nearly five o'clock when the picnic party was finally ready to start for its junketing.

Mrs Blackwood had arrived, bringing her two promised young men, Ted Landon and John Clark.

Rearrayed in picnic garb, the house guests were ready for the fun, and the Frederick Varians were getting together and looking over the baskets of supper.

"If we could only have kept one helper by us," bemoaned Minna Varian, her speech accompanied by her usual wringing of her distressed hands. "I begged Kelly to stay but he wouldn't."

"The circus is here only one day, you know, Mrs. Varian," Landon told her, "and I fancy every servant in Headland Harbor has gone to it. But command me "

"Indeed, we will," put in Betty; "carry this, please, and, Uncle Herbert, you take this coffee paraphernalia."

Divided among the willing hands, the luggage was not too burdensome, and the cavalcade prepared to start.

"No fear of burglars, I take it," said Herbert, as his brother closed the front door and shook it to be sure it was fastened.

"Not a bit," and Frederick Varian took up his own baskets. "No one can possibly reach this house, save through that gate down by the lodge. And that is locked. Also the windows and doors of the house are all fastened. So if you people have left jewelry on your dressing tables, don't be alarmed, you'll find it there on your return."

"All aboard!" shouted Landon, and they started by twos or threes, but in a moment were obliged to walk single file down the steep and narrow path.

"Oh, my heavens!" cried Betty, suddenly, "I must go back! I've forgotten my camera. Let me take your key, Father, I'll run and get it in a minute!"

"I'll go and get it for you, Betty," said Varian, setting down his burden.

"No, Dad, you can't; it's in a closet, behind a lot of other things, and you'd upset the whole lot into a dreadful mess. I know you!"

"Let me go, Miss Varian," offered several of the others, but Bettywas insistent.

"No one can get it but myself,—at least, not without a lot of delay and trouble. Give me the key, Father, I'll be right back."

"But, Betty—"

"Oh, give her the key, Fred!" exclaimed his wife; "don't torment the child! I believe you enjoy teasing her! There, take the key, Betty, and run along. Hurry, do, for it's annoying to have to wait for you."

"Let me go with you," asked John Clark, but Betty smiled a refusal and ran off alone.

Most of them watched the lithe, slight figure, as she bounded up the rugged, irregular steps, sometimes two of them at a time, and at last they saw her fitting the key into the front door.

She called back a few words, but the distance was too great for them to hear her clearly, although they could see her.

She waved her hand, smilingly, and disappeared inside the house, leaving the door wide open behind her.

"Extraordinary place!" Herbert Varian said, taking in the marvelous crag from this new viewpoint.

"You must see it from the clubhouse," said Landon; "can't you all come here tomorrow afternoon, on my invite?"

"We'll see," Mrs. Varian smiled at him, for it was impossible not to like this frank, good looking youth. The conversation was entirely of the wonders and beauties of Headland House, until at last, Mrs. Blackwood said, "Isn't that child gone a long while? I could have found half a dozen cameras by this time!"

"She is a long time," Frederick Varian said, frowning; "I was just thinking that myself. I think I'll go after her."

"No, don't," said his wife, nervously, "you'll get into an argument with her, and never get back! Let her alone,— she'll be here in a minute."

But the minutes went by, and Betty didn't reappear in the open doorway.

"I know what she's up to," and Frederick Varian shook his head, in annoyance.

Whereupon Mrs. Frederick began to cry.

"Now, Fred, stop," she said; "Herbert, you go up to the house and tell Betty to come along. If she can't find her camera, tell her to come without it. I wish we had a megaphone so we could call her. Go on, Herbert."

"Stay where you are, Herbert," said his brother "I shall go. It's all right, Minna, I won't tease the child,—I promise you. It's all right, dear."

He kissed his wife lightly on the brow, and started off at a swinging pace up the rocky flight of steps.

"I'll fetch her," he called back, as he proceeded beyond hearing distance. "Chirk up, Minna, Janet; tell her I shan't abuse Betty."

"What does he mean by that?" asked Mrs. Herbert of Mrs. Frederick, as she repeated the message.

"Oh, nothing," and Mrs. Frederick clasped her hands resignedly. "Only you know how Betty and her father are always more or less at odds. I don't know why it is,— they're devoted to each other, yet they're always quarreling."

"They don't mean anything," and her sister in law smiled. "I know them both, and they're an ideal father and daughter."

CHAPTER 3: THE TRAGEDY

DOCTOR HERBERT VARIAN stood slightly apart from the rest of the group, his observant eyes taking in all the details of the peculiar situation of his brother's house. His eye traversed back over the short distance they had already come, and he saw a narrow, winding and exceedingly steep path. At intervals it was a succession of broken, irregular steps, rocky and sharp-edged. Again, it would be a fairly easy, though stony footway. But it led to the house, and had no branch or side track in any direction.

"Everything and everybody that comes to this house has to come by this path?" he demanded.

"Yes," said Minna Varian, and added, complainingly, "a most disagreeable arrangement. All the servants and tradespeople have to use it as well as ourselves and our guests."

"That could be remedied," suggested Varian, "a branch, say—"

"We'll never do it," said Minna, sharply. "I don't like the place well enough to buy it, though that is what Fred has in mind—"

"No, don't buy it," advised her brother in law. "I see nothing in its favor except its wonderful beauty and strange, weird charm. That's a good deal, I admit, but not enough for a comfortable summer home."

He turned and gazed out over the open sea. From the high headland the view was unsurpassable. The few nearby boats seemed lost in the great expanse of waters. Some chugging motor boats and a dozen or so sailing craft ventured not very far from shore. North, along the Maine coast, he saw only more rocky promontories and rockbound inlets.

Turning slowly toward the South, he saw the graceful curve of Headland Harbor, with its grouped village houses and spreading array of summer cottages.

"I never saw anything finer," he declared. "I almost think, Minna, after all, you would be wise to buy the place, and then, arrange to make it more getatable. A continuous flight of strong wooden steps—"

"Would spoil the whole thing!" exclaimed Claire Blackwood. "Oh, Doctor Varian, don't propose anything like that! We Harborers love this place, just as it is, and we would defend it against any such innovations. I think there's a law about defacing natural scenery."

"Don't bother," said Minna, carelessly; "we'll never do anything of the sort. I won't agree to it."

"That's right," said her sister in law. "This is no place to bring up Betty. The girl has no real society here, no advantages, no scope. She'll become a savage—"

"Not Betty," Minna Varian laughed. "She's outdoor loving and all that, but she has nothing of the barbarian in her. I think she'd like to go to a far gayer resort. But her father—"

"Where is her father?" asked Doctor Varian, impatiently. "It will be dark before we get to our picnic. Why don't they come?"

He gave a loud view halloo, but only the echoes from the rocky heights answered him.

"I knew it!" and Minna Varian began to wring her hands. "He and Betty are quarreling,—I am sure of it!"

"What do you mean, Min? What's this quarreling business about?"

"They've always done it,—it's nothing new. They adore each other, but they're eternally disagreeing and fighting it out. They're quite capable of forgetting all about us, and arguing out some foolish subject while we sit here waiting for them!"

"I'll go and stir them up," the doctor said, starting in the direction of the house.

"Oh, no, Herbert. It's a hard climb, and you've enough walking ahead of you."

"I'll go," and Ted Landon looked inquiringly at Mrs. Varian.

"Oh, what's the use?" she said; "they'll surely appear in a minute."

So they all waited a few minutes longer and then Janet Varian spoke up.

"I think it's a shame to keep us here like this. Go on up to the house, Mr. Landon, do. Tell those two foolish people that they must come on or the picnic will proceed without them."

"All right," said Ted, and began sprinting over the rocks.

"I'm going, too," and Claire Blackwood followed Landon.

"We may as well all go, and have our picnic on our own verandah," said Minna, complainingly, and though Doctor Varian would have preferred that to any further exertions, he did not say so.

"It's always like this," Minna's querulous voice went on; "whenever we start to go anywhere, somebody has to go back for something and they're so slow and so inconsiderate of other people's feelings—"

"There they go," interrupted Doctor Varian as the two latest emissaries went up over the rocks. "Now the house will swallow them up!"

"Oh, Herbert, don't say such awful things," wailed Minna; "you sound positively creepy! I have a feeling of fear of that house anyway,—I believe it would like to swallow people up!"

"Ought we to intrude?" Claire Blackwood laughingly asked of Landon, as they neared the house; "if Betty and her father want to quarrel, they ought to be allowed to do so in peace."

"Oh, well, if they insist, we'll go away again, and let them have it out comfortably. Queer thing, for Daughter and Dad to make a habit of scrapping!"

"I take Mrs. Varian's statements with a grain of salt," said Claire, sagely. "She's not awfully well balanced, that woman, and I doubt if Betty and her father are half as black as they're painted. Shall we ring the bell or walk right in?"

But this question needed no answer, for as they mounted the steps of the verandah and neared the open front door, they were confronted by the sight of Mr. Frederick Varian sprawled at full length on the floor of the hall.

"Oh, heavens, what is the matter?" cried Claire; "the man has had a stroke or something!"

Landon went nearer, and with a grave face, stooped down to the prostrate figure.

"Claire," he whispered, looking up at her with a white face, "Claire, this man is dead."

"What? No,—no! it can't be—"

"Yes, he is,—I'm almost certain,—I don't think I'd better touch him,—or, should I? It can do no harm to feel for his heart,—no, it is not beating,—what does it mean? Where's Miss Varian?"

"Think quickly, Mr. Landon, what we ought to do." Claire Blackwood spoke earnestly, and tried to pull herself together. "We must be careful to do the right thing. I should say, before we even think of Miss Betty we should call Doctor Varian up here—"

"The very thing! Will you call him, or shall I?" Considerately, Landon gave her her choice.

With a shuddering glance at the still figure, Claire said, "You call him, but let me go with you."

They stepped out on the veranda, and Landon waved his hand at the group of waiting people below him.

Then he beckoned, but no one definitely responded.

"I'll have to shout," Ted said, with a regretful look. "Somehow I hate to," the presence of death seemed to restrain him.

But of necessity, he called out, "Doctor Varian,—come here."

The distance was almost too far for his voice to carry, but because of his imperative gestures, Herbert Varian said: "Guess I'll have to go. Lord! What can be the trick they're trying to cut up? I vow I won't come back here! I'll eat my picnic in your dining room, Minna."

"As you like," she returned, indifferently. "I hate picnics, anyway. But for goodness' sake, Herbert, do one thing or the other. If you'd really rather not go to the woods, take your baskets, and we'll all go back to the house. It's getting late, anyway."

"Wait a bit," counseled the doctor. "You people stay here, till I go up to the house, and see what's doing. Then if I beckon you, come along back, all of you. If I don't break my neck getting up there!"

"Don't go, Father," begged Eleanor; "let me go. What in the world can they want of you?"

"No,—I'll go. I suppose there's a leak in the pipes or something."

Herbert Varian went off at a gait that belied his recalcitrant attitude, and as he neared the house, he could see the white faces and grave air of the two that awaited him.

"What's the great idea?" he called out, cheerily.

"A serious matter, Doctor Varian," replied Landon. "An accident, or sudden illness—"

"No!" the doctor took the remaining steps at a bound. "Who?"

For answer, Landon conducted him inside the hall, and in an instant Varian was on his knees beside the stricken man.

"My God!" he said, in a hoarse whisper, "Frederick's dead!"

"A stroke?" asked Landon, while Claire Blackwood stood by, unable to speak at all.

"No, man, no! Shot! See the blood,—shot through the heart. What does it—what can it mean? Where's Betty?"

"We don't know," Claire spoke now. "Doctor Varian, are you sure he's dead? Can nothing be done to save him?"

"Nothing. He died almost instantly, from internal hemorrhage. But how unbelievable! How impossible!"

"Who shot him?" Landon burst out, impetuously; "or,—is it suicide?"

"Where's the pistol?" said the doctor, looking about.

Both men searched, Landon trying to overcome his repugnance to such close association with the dead, but no weapon of any sort could be found.

"I—I can't see it,—" Varian wiped his perspiring brow. "I can't see any solution. But, this won't do. We must get the others up here. Oh, heavens, what shall we do with Minna?"

"Let me go down, and take her home with me," suggested Claire Blackwood, eager to do anything that might help or ease the coming disclosure of the tragedy.

"Oh, I don't know,—" demurred Varian. "You see, she's got to know,—of course, she must be told at once,—and then,—she'll have to look after Betty, —where is the child? Anyway, my wife is a tower of strength,—she'll be able to manage Mrs. Varian, —even if she has violent hysterics,—which, of course, she will!"

"Command me, Doctor Varian," said Landon. "I will do whatever you advise."

"All right; I'll be glad of your assistance. Suppose you go back to the people down there on the rocks, and then,—let me see,—suppose you tell my wife first what has happened; then, ask her to break the news to Mrs. Varian,—she'll know how best to do it. Then,—oh, Lord,—I don't know what then! They'll have to come back here,—I suppose,—what else can they do? I don't know, Mrs. Blackwood, but your idea of taking Mrs. Varian away with you is a good one. If she'll go."

"She won't go," said Claire, decidedly, "if she knows the truth. If I take her, it'll have to be on some false pretense,—"

"Won't do," said Varian, briefly. "We've got no right to keep her in ignorance of her husband's death. No; she must be told. That girl of mine, too,—Eleanor, she hasn't her mother's poise,—she's likely to go to pieces,—always does, in the presence of death. Oh, what a moil!"

"Here's another thing," said Landon, a little hesitantly. "What about the authorities?"

"Yes,—yes,—" the doctor spoke impatiently, "I thought of that,—who are they, in this God forsaken place? Town Constable, I suppose."

"I don't know myself," said Landon. "County Sheriff, more likely. But Clark's a good, sensible sort. Say we send him down to the village—"

"Oh, must it be known down there right away?" cried Claire. "Before even Mrs. Varian is told! Or Betty. Where *is* Betty?"

"Betty is somewhere in the house," said Doctor Varian in a low voice. "We know that. Now, let that question rest, till we decide on our first move. I think, Landon, you'd better do as I said. Go and tell my wife, and, while she's telling Mrs. Varian and my daughter, Eleanor, you can take Mr. Clarke aside and tell him. Then,—then, I think, you'd all better come back here to the house. We'll send Clark on that errand later,—or, we can telephone."

Landon started on his difficult descent and on his even more difficult errand.

"Can't you,—can't you put Mr. Varian somewhere — somewhere—" Claire began, incoherently.

"I'm not supposed to move a body until the authorities give permission," said Doctor Varian, slowly. "It would seem to me, that in this very peculiar and unusual case, that I might,—but, that's just it. I've been thinking,—and the very mysteriousness of this thing, makes it most necessary for me to be unusually circumspect. Why, Mrs. Blackwood, have you any idea what we have ahead of us? I can't think this mystery will be simple or easily explained. I don't "

"What do you think—"

"I don't dare think! Isn't there a phrase, 'that way madness lies'? Well, it recurs to me when I let myself think! No,—I won't think,—and I beg of you, don't question me! I'm not a hysterical woman,—but there are times when a man feels as if hysterics might be a relief!"

"Then let's not think,—" said Claire, tactfully, "but let me try to be helpful. If Mrs. Varian is coming here,— do you advise that we—cover—Mr Varian with—"

"With a sheet, I suppose,—do you know where to find one?"

"No, I've never been upstairs,—and then, after all, isn't a sheet even more gruesome than the sight as it is at present? How about a dark cover?"

"Very well,—find one." The Doctor spoke absorbedly, uncaring.

Glancing about, Claire noticed a folded steamer rug, on the end of the big davenport in the hall, and fetching that, she laid it lightly over the still form.

"Now, about Betty,—" said the doctor, coming out of his brown study. "She is in the house,—probably hiding,—from fear,—"

"Oh, do you think that? Then let us find her!"

"We can't both go. Will you remain here and meet the others or shall I stay here while you go to look for the girl?"

Claire Blackwood pondered. Either suggestion was too hard for her to accept.

"I can't, " she said, at last. "I'm a coward, I suppose,— but I can't search this great, empty house,—for Betty. And, if she were in it, she would surely come here to us."

Doctor Varian looked at her.

"Then I'll go," he said, simply. "You stay here."

"No!" Claire grasped his arm. "I can't do that either. Oh, Doctor Varian, stay here with me! Think,—these are not my people,—I'm sympathetic, of course, but, I'm terrified,—I'm afraid—"

"There's nothing to fear."

"I can't help that,—I won't stay here alone. If you leave me, I shall run down the path to meet them."

"Then I'll have to stay here. Very well, Mrs. Blackwood, they'll arrive in a few moments,—we'll wait for them together."

And then Varian again fell to ruminating, and Claire Blackwood, sick with her own thoughts, said no word.

At last they heard footsteps, and looked out to see the little procession headed by the two sisters in law.

Janet Varian was half supporting Minna, but her help was not greatly needed, for the very violence of Minna's grief and fright gave her a sort of supernormal strength and she walked uprightly and swiftly.

"Where's Frederick?" she demanded, in a shrill voice as she came up the steps,—"and where's Betty? Where's my child?"

Her voice rose to a shriek on the last words, and Doctor Varian took her by the arm, giving her his undivided attention.

"Be careful now, Minna," he said, kindly but decidedly; "don't lose your grip. You've a big trouble to face,—and do try, dear, to meet it bravely."

"I'm brave enough, Herbert, don't worry about that. Where's Fred, I say?"

"Here," was the brief reply, and Varian led her to her husband's body.

As he had fully expected, she went into violent hysterics. She cried, she screamed, then her voice subsided to a sort of low, dismal wailing, only to break out afresh with renewed shrieks.

"Perhaps it's better that she should do this, than to control herself," the Doctor said; "she'll soon exhaust herself at this rate, and may in that way become more tractable. I wish we could get her to bed."

"We can," responded his wife, promptly. "I'll look after that. Give a look at Eleanor, Herbert."

The harassed doctor turned his attention to his daughter, who was controlliug herself, but who was trembling piteously.

"Good girl," said her father, taking her in his arms. "Buck up, Nell, dear. Dad's got a whole lot on his shoulders, and my, how it will help if you don't keel over!"

"I won't," and Eleanor tried to smile. Claire Blackwood approached the pair.

"Doctor Varian," she said, "suppose I take your daughter home with me for the night,—or longer, if she'll stay. It might relieve you and your wife of a little care, and I'll be good to her, I promise you. And, if I may, I'd like to go now. I can't be of any service here, can I? And as Miss Eleanor can't either, what do you think of our going now?"

"A very good idea, Mrs. Blackwood," and the doctor's face showed grateful appreciation. "Take one of the young men with you, and leave the other here

to help me."

"We'll take John Clark," Claire decided, "and Ted Landon will, I know, be glad to stand by you."

The three departed, and then the sisters in law left the room and went upstairs, Minna making no resistance to Janet's suggestions.

Left alone with the dead, Doctor Varian and young Landon looked at each other.

"What does it all mean?" asked the younger man, a look of absolute bewilderment on his face.

"I can't make it out," returned the other, slowly. "But it's a pretty awful situation. Now the women are gone, I'll speak out the thing that troubles me most. Where's Betty?"

"Who? Miss Varian? Why, yes, where is she? She came for her camera, you know. She—why, she must be in the house."

"She must be,—that is,—I can't see any alternative. I understand there's no way out of this house, save down the path we took."

"No other, sir."

"Then if the girl's in the house,—she must be found."

"Yes," and Landon saw the terrible fear in the other's eyes, and his own glance responded.

"Shall we search the rooms?"

"That must be done. Now, I'm not willing to leave the body of my brother unattended. Will you watch by it, while I run over the house, or the other way about?"

"I'll do as you prefer I should, Doctor Varian,—but if you give me a choice, I'll stay here. I've never been in the house before, and I don't know the rooms. However, I want to be frank,—and, the truth is, I'd rather not make that search,—even if I did know the rooms."

"I understand, Mr. Landon, and I don't blame you. I've never been in the house before either,—and I don't at all like the idea of the search, but it must be made,—and made at once, and it's my place to do it. So, then, if you'll remain here, I'll go the rounds."

Ted Landon nodded silently, and sat down to begin the vigil he had been asked to keep.

Herbert Varian went first upstairs to Minna's room, and opening the door softly, discovered the widow was lying quietly on her bed. Janet, sitting by, placed a warning forefinger against her lip, and seeing that the patient was quiet, Varian noiselessly closed the door and tiptoed away.

He stood a moment in the second story hall, looking upward at a closed door, to which a narrow and winding staircase would take him.

Should he go up there,—or search the two lower stories first? He looked out of a window at the foot of the little stair.

It gave West, and afforded no view of the sea. But the wild and inaccessible rocks which he saw, proved to him finally that there was no way of approach to this lonely house, save by that one and only path he had already climbed. He sighed, for this dashed his last hope that

Betty might have left the house on some errand or some escapade before her father had reached it.

With vague forebodings and a horrible sinking at his heart, he began to ascend the turret stair.

CHAPTER 4: THE SEARCH

DOCTOR HERBERT VARIAN was a man accustomed to responsibilities; more, he was accustomed to the responsibilities of other people as well as his own. Yet it seemed to him that the position in which he now found himself was more appalling than anything he had ever before experienced, and that it was liable to grow worse rather than better with successive developments.

Varian had what has been called "the leaping mind," and without being unduly apprehensive, he saw trouble ahead, such as he shuddered to think about. His brother dead, there was the hysterical widow to be cared for. And Betty in hiding–

He paused, his hand on the latch of the door at the top of the stair.

Then, squaring his shoulders, he shook off his hesitation and opened the door.

He found himself in a small turret room, from which he went on to other rooms on that floor. They were, for the most part, quite evidently unoccupied bedrooms, but two gave signs of being in use by servants.

Varian paid little heed to his surroundings, but went rapidly about hunting for the missing girl.

"Betty,—" he called, softly; "Betty, dear, where are you? Don't be afraid,—Uncle Herbert will take care of you. Come, Betty, come out of hiding."

But there was no answer to his calls. He flung open cupboard doors, he peered into dark corners and alcoves, but he saw no trace of any one, nor heard any sound.

Two other tiny staircases led up to higher turrets, but these were empty, and search as he would he found no Betty, nor any trace of her.

Unwilling to waste what might be valuable time, Doctor Varian went downstairs again.

Then, one after another, he visited all the rooms on the second floor but found no sign of his niece.

He went again to the room where the women were and beckoned his wife outside.

"Minna is asleep?" he asked, in a whisper.

"Yes," Janet replied, "but, of course, only as an effect of that strong opiate you gave her. She tosses and moans,—but, yes, she is asleep."

"I dread her waking. What *are* we to do with her? And, Janet, where is Betty? I've been all over these upper floors,—and now I'll tackle the rooms downstairs, and the cellar. The girl must be found—"

"Herbert! Did you ever know such a fearful situation? And—as to—Frederick—don't you have to–"

"Yes, yes, of course; the authorities must be called in. Don't think I haven't realized that. But first of all we must find Betty—dead or alive!"

"Don't say that!" Janet clutched at his arm. "I can't bear any more horrors."

"Poor girl,—you may have to. Brace up, dear, I've all I can do to—"

"Of course you have," his wife kissed him tenderly. "Don't be afraid. I won't add to your burdens, and I will help all I can. Thank heaven that kind woman took Eleanor away with her."

"Yes; but I daresay we ought to have kept them all here. There's crime to be considered, and—"

"Never mind, they're gone,—and I'm glad of it. You can get them back when necessary."

"But it's a mystery,—oh, what shall I do first? I never felt so absolutely unable to cope with a situation. But the first thing is to hunt further for Betty."

Pursuant of his clearest duty, Doctor Varian went on through the yet unsearched rooms, on to the kitchen, and on down to the cellar. He made a hasty but careful search, flinging open closets, cupboards and storerooms, and returned at last to the hall where Ted Landon sat with folded arms, keeping his lonely vigil.

"I can't imagine where Betty can be," and Varian sank wearily into a chair.

"She must be in the house," said Landon, wonderingly, "for there's no way out, except down the path where we all were."

"There's a back door, I suppose."

"I mean no way off the premises. Yes, there must be a back door—you know I've never been in this house before."

"No; well, look here, Landon; the authorities must be notified; the local doctor ought to be called in,—and all that. But first, I want to find Betty. Suppose I stay here,—I'm—I admit I'm pretty tired, —and you take a look out around the back door, and kitchen porch. By the way, the servants will be coming home soon—"

"No, they were to stay out for the evening, I thing Mrs. Varian said."

"But those people who went back to the village will, of course, tell of the matter, and soon we'll have all kinds of curious visitors."

"All right, Doctor Varian, I'll do just what you say."

"The younger man went on his errand, and going through the kitchen, found the back porch. To reach it he had to unlock the outside door, thus proving to his own satisfaction that Betty had not gone out that way.

But he went out and looked about. He saw nothing indicative. The porch was pleasant and in neat order. A knitting bag and a much be thumbed novel were evidently the property of the cook or waitress, and an old cap on a nail was, doubtless, the butler's.

He took pains to ascertain that there was no path or road that led down to the gate but the path that also went from the front door, and which he had been on when Betty returned to the house.

He had seen her enter the house, had seen her father go in a few moments later, now where was the girl?

Back to the kitchen Landon went, and in the middle of the floor, he noticed a yellow cushion. It was a satin covered, embroidered affair, probably, he thought, a sofa cushion, or hammock pillow, but it seemed too elaborate for a servant's cushion. Surely it belonged to the family.

The kitchen was in tidy order, save for a tray of used glasses and empty plates which was on a table.

Landon picked up the pillow,—and then, on second thoughts, laid it back where he had found it. It might be evidence.

An open door showed the cellar stairs. Conquering a strong disinclination, Landon went down. The cellar was large, and seemed to have various rooms and bins, and some locked cupboards. But there was nothing sinister, the rooms were for the most part fairly light, and the air was good.

Remembering that Doctor Varian had already searched down there for Betty, Landon merely went over the same ground, and returned with the news of his unsuccessful search.

"No way out?" queried the doctor, briefly.

"None, except by passing the very spot where we all were when Betty ran back to the house."

"Where is she, Landon?"

The two men stared at each other, both absolutely at a loss to answer the question.

"Well," and Varian pulled himself together, "this won't do. It's a case for the police,—how shall we get at them?"

"I don't know anything about the police, but if you telephone the inn or the clubhouse they'll tell you. The local doctor is Merritt,—I know him. But he couldn't do anything. Why call him when you're here?"

"It's customary, I think. You call Merritt, will you, and then I'll speak to the innkeeper."

The telephoning was just about completed, when a fearful scream from upstairs announced the fact that Minna Varian had awakened from her opiate sleep and had returned to a realization of her troubles.

Slowly Doctor Varian rose and went up the stairs.

He entered the bedroom to find Minna sitting up in bed, wild eyed and struggling to get up, while Janet urged her to lie still.

"Lie still!" she screamed, "I will not. Come here, Herbert. Tell me,—where is my child? Why is Betty not here? Is she dead, too? Tell me, I say!"

"Yes, Minna," Varian returned, quietly, "I will tell you all I can. I do not know where Betty is; but we've no reason to think she is dead—"

"Then why doesn't she come to me? Why doesn't Fred come? Oh,—Fred is dead,—isn't he?"

And then the poor woman went into violent hysterics, now shrieking like a maniac and now moaning piteously, like some hurt animal.

"The first thing to do," said Doctor Varian, decidedly, "is to get a nurse for Minna."

"No," demurred his wife, "not tonight, anyway. I'll take care of her, and there will be some maid servant who can help me. There was a nice looking waitress among those who went off this afternoon."

"The servants will surely return as soon as they hear the news," Varian said, and then he gave all his attention to calming his patient.

Again he placed her under the influence of a powerful opiate, and by the time she was unconscious, the local doctor had come.

Varian went down to find Doctor Merritt examining the body of his brother.

The two medical men met courteously, the local doctor assuming an important air, principally because he considered the other his superior.

"Terrible thing, Doctor Varian," Merritt said; "death practically instantaneous."

"Practically," returned the other. "May have lived a few moments, but unconscious at once. You know the sheriff?"

"Yes; Potter. He'll be along soon. He's a shrewd one,—but,—my heavens! Who did this thing?"

Doctor Merritt's formality gave way before his irrepressible curiosity. He looked from Doctor Varian to Ted Landon and back again, with an exasperated air of resentment at being told so little.

"We don't know, Doctor Merritt," London said, as the other doctor said nothing. "We've no idea."

"No idea! A man shot and killed in this lonely, isolated house and you don't know who did it? What do you mean?"

In a few words Varian detailed the circumstances, and added, "We don't know where Miss Varian is."

"Disappeared! Then she must have shot her father—"

"Oh, no!" interrupted Landon, "don't say such an absurd thing!"

"What else is there to say?" demanded Merritt. "You say there was nobody in the house but those two people. Now, one is here dead, and the other is missing. What else can be said?"

"Don't accuse a defenseless girl,—" advised Varian. "Betty must be found, of course. But I don't for a minute believe she shot her father."

"Where's the gun?" asked Doctor Merritt.

"Hasn't been found," returned Varian, briefly. "Mrs Varian, my brother's wife, is hysterical. I've been obliged to quiet her by opiates. Doctor Merritt, this is by no means a simple case. I hope your sheriff is a man of brains and experience. It's going to call for wise and competent handling."

"Potter is experienced enough. Been sheriff for years. But as to brains, he isn't overburdened with them. Still, he's got good horse sense."

"One of the best things to have," commented Varian. "Now, I don't know that we need keep Mr. Landon here any longer. What do you think?"

"I don't know," said Merritt, thoughtfully. "He was here at the time of the—crime?"

"Yes; but so were several others, and they've gone away. As you like, Mr. Landon, but I don't think you need stay unless you wish."

"I do wish," Ted Landon said. "I may be of use, somehow, and, too, I'm deeply interested. I want to see what the sheriff thinks about it, and, too, I want to try to find or help to find Miss Betty."

"Betty must be found," said Varian, as if suddenly reminded of the fact. "I am so distracted between the shock of my brother's death and the anxiety regarding his wife's condition, that for the moment I almost forgot Betty. That child must be hiding somewhere. She must have been frightened in some fearful way, and either fainted or run away and hid out in the grounds somewhere. I'm positive she isn't in the house."

"She couldn't have gone out the back door," said Landon. "It was locked when I went to it."

"She couldn't have gone out at the front door or we should have seen her," Varian added, "She stepped out of a window, then."

"Are you assuming some intruder?" asked Merritt, wonderingly.

"I'm not assuming anything," returned Varian, a little crisply, for his nerves were on edge. "But Betty Varian must be found,—my duty is to the living as well as to the dead."

He glanced at his brother's body, and his face expressed a mute promise to care for that brother's child.

"But how are you going to find her?" asked Landon. "We saw Miss Varian enter this house—"

"Therefore, she is still in it,—or in the grounds," said Varian, positively. "It can't be otherwise. I shall hunt out of doors first, before it grows dusk. Then we can hunt the house afterward."

"You have hunted the house."

"Yes; but it must be hunted more thoroughly. Why, Betty, or—Betty's body must be somewhere. And must be found."

Doctor Merritt listened, dumfounded. Here was mystery indeed. Mr. Varian dead,—shot,—no weapon found, and his daughter missing. What could be the explanation?

The hunt out of doors for Betty resulted in nothing at all. There was no kitchen garden, merely a drying plot and a small patch of back yard, mostly stones and hard ground. This was surrounded by dwarfed and stunted pine trees, which not only afforded no hiding place, but shut off no possible nook or cranny where Betty could be hidden. The whole tableland was exposed to view from all parts of it, and it was clear to be seen that Betty Varian could not be hiding out of doors.

And since she could not have left the premises, save by the road where the picnic party was congregated, there was no supposition but that she was still in the house.

"Can you form any theory, Doctor Varian?" Landon asked him.

"No, I can't. Can you?"

"Only the obvious one,—that Miss Varian killed her father and then hid somewhere."

"But where? Mind you, I don't for a moment admit she killed her father, that's too ridiculous! But whoever killed him, may also have killed her. It is her body I think we are more likely to find."

"How, then, did the assassin get away?"

"I don't know. I'm not prepared to say there's no way out of this place—"

"But I know that to be the fact. There comes the sheriff, Doctor Varian. That's Potter."

They went into the house again, and found the sheriff and another man with him.

Merritt made the necessary introductions, and Doctor Varian looked at Potter.

"The strangest case you've ever had," he informed him, "and the most important. How do you propose to handle it?"

"Like I do all the others, by using my head."

"Yes, I know, but I mean what help do you expect to have?"

"Dunno's I'll need any yet. Haven't got the principal facts. Dead man's your brother, ain't he?"

"Yes."

"Shot dead and no weapon around. Criminal unknown. Now, about this young lady,—the daughter. Where is she?"

"I don't know,—but I hope you can find her."

And then Doctor Varian told, in his straightforward way, of his search for the girl.

"Mighty curious," vouchsafed the sheriff, with an air of one stating a new idea. "The girl and her father on good terms?"

"Yes, of course," Varian answered, but his slight hesitation made the sheriff eye him keenly.

"We want the truth, you know," he said, thoughtfully. "If them two wasn't on good terms, you might as well say so,—'cause it'll come out sooner or later."

"But they were,—so far as I know."

"Oh, well, all right. I can't think yet, the girl shot her father. I won't think that,—lessen I have to. But, good land, man, you say you've looked all over the house,— where's the murderer, then?"

"Suicide?" laconically said the man who had come with the sheriff.

It was the first time he had spoken. He was a quiet, insignificant chap, but his eyes were keen and his whole face alert.

"Couldn't be, Bill," said the sheriff, "with no weapon about."

"Might 'a' been removed," the other said, in his brief way.

"By whom?" asked Doctor Varian.

"By whoever came here first," Bill returned, looking at him.

"I came here first," Varian stated. "Do you mean I removed the weapon?"

"Have to look at all sides, you know."

"Well, I didn't. But I won't take time, now, to enlarge on that plain statement. I'll be here, you can question me, when and as often as you like. Now, Mr. Potter, what are you going to do first?"

"Well, seems to me there's no more to be done with Mr. Varian's body. You two doctors have examined it, you know all about the wound that killed him. Bill, here, has jotted down all the details of its position and all that. Now, I think you can call in the undertakers and have the body taken away or kept here till the funeral,—whichever you like."

"The funeral!" exclaimed Doctor Varian, realizing a further responsibility for his laden shoulders. "I suppose I'd better arrange about that, for my sister in law will not be able to do so."

"Jest 's you like," said Potter. "Next, I'll investigate for myself the absence of this girl. A mysterious disappearance is as serious a matter as a mysterious death,—maybe, more so."

"That's true," agreed Varian. "I hope you'll be able to find my niece, for she must be found."

"Easy enough to say she must be found,—the trick is to find her."

"Have you any theory of the crime, Mr. Potter?" Landon asked.

"Theory? No, I don't deal in theories. I may say it looks to me like the girl may have shot her father, but it only looks that way because there's no other way, so far, for it to look. You can't suspect a criminal that you ain't had any hint of, can If anybody, now, turns up who's seen a man prowling round—or seen any mysterious person, or if any servant is found who, say, didn't go to the circus, but hung behind, or—"

"But if there's any such, they or he must be in the house now," Bill said, quietly. "Let's go and see."

The two started from the room and Landon, after a glance at Doctor Varian, followed them.

"I don't see," Landon said to Potter as they went to the kitchen, "why you folks in authority always seem to think it necessary to take an antagonistic attitude toward the people who are representing the dead man! You act toward Doctor Varian as if you more than half suspected he had a hand in the crime himself!"

"Not that, my boy," and Potter looked at him gravely; "but that doctor brother knows more than he's telling."

"That's not so! I know. I came up here to the house with him. I was with him when he found his brother's body "

"Oh, you were! Why didn't you say so?"

"You didn't ask me. No, I don't know anything more. I've nothing to tell that can throw any possible light, but I do know that Doctor Varian had no hand in it and knows no more about it than I do."

"Good land, I don't mean that he killed his brother,—I know better than that. But he wasn't frank about the relations between the girl and her father Do you know that they were all right? Friendly, I mean?"

"So far as I know, they were. But I never met them until today. I can only say that they acted like any normal, usual father and daughter."

"Oh, well, it doesn't matter. It'll all come out,—that sort of thing. Now to find the girl."

Chapter 5: The Yellow Pillow

WHAT'S this pillow doing here?" the sheriff asked, as he picked up the yellow satin cushion. "This looks to me like a parlor ornament."

"I thought it was strange, too," returned Landon. "But I can't see any clue in it, can you?"

"Anything unusual may prove a clue," said Potter, sententiously. You never saw this pillow before, Mr. Landon."

"No; but I'm not familiar with the house at all. Maybe it's a discarded one, handed down to the servants' use."

"Doesn't look so; it's fresh and new, and very handsome."

"Lay it aside and come on," growled Bill Dunn, who was alertly looking about the kitchen. "You can ask the family about that later. Let's go down cellar."

To the cellar they went, Landon following. He had a notion that he might help the family's interests by keeping at the heels of these detectives.

But the most careful search revealed nothing of importance to their quest.

Until Potter said, suddenly, "What's this? A well?"

"It sure is," and Bill Dunn peered over an old well curb and looked down.

"A well in a cellar! How queer!" exclaimed Landon. "I never heard of such a thing."

"Uncommon, but I've known of 'em," said Bill. "Looks promising, eh?"

Potter considered. "It may mean something," he said, thoughtfully. "We'll have to sound it, somehow."

"Sound it, nothin'!" said the executive Bill; "I'll go down."

"How?" Potter asked him. "There's no bucket. It's probably a dried up well."

"Prob'ly," and Bill nodded. He already had one foot over the broken old well curb.

"Wait, for heaven's sake!" cried Landon. "Don't jump down! You must have a light."

"Got one," and Bill drew a small flashlight from his pocket.

With the agility of a monkey he clambered down the side of the old well. The stones were large and not smoothly fitted, so that he had little trouble in gaining and keeping his foothold.

The others watched him as he descended and at last reached the bottom.

"Nothing at all," he called up. "I'm coming back."

"Just an old dried up well," he reported, as he reached them again. "Must 'a' dried up long ago. No water in it for years, most likely. But there's nothin' else down there, neither. No body, nor no clues of any sort. Whatever became of that girl, she ain't down that well."

All parts of the cellar were subjected to the same thorough search.

Landon was amazed at the quickness and efficiency shown by these men whom he had thought rather stupid at first.

Cupboards were poked into to their furthest corners; bins were raked; boxes opened, and Bill even climbed up to scan a swinging shelf that hung above his head.

"How about secret passages?" Potter asked, when they had exhausted all obvious hiding places.

"I been thinkin' about that," Bill returned, musingly; "but, so far, I can't see where there could be any. This isn't the sort of house that has 'em, either. It's straightforward architecture,—that's what it is,— straightforward."

"What do you mean by that?" asked Landon, interested in this strange man who looked so ignorant, yet was in some ways so well informed.

"Well, you see, there's no unexpected juts or jambs. Everything's four square, mostly. You can see where the rooms above are,—you can see where the closets and stairs fit in and all that. There's no concealed territory like,—no real chance for a secret passage,—at least not so far's I see."

"That's right," agreed Potter. "Bill's the man when it comes to architecture and building plans. Well,—let's get along upstairs, then."

Going through the kitchen again, Potter picked up the yellow pillow and took it along with him. Quite evidently it belonged to a sofa in the large, square front hall. The upholstery fabric was the same, and there was a corresponding pillow already at one end of the sofa.

"Queer thing," Potter said; "how'd that fine cushion get on the kitchen floor?"

"It is queer," Landon assented, "but I can't see any meaning in it, can you?"

"Not yet," returned Potter. "Now, Doctor Varian," and he turned to the physician who sat. with bowed head beside his brother's body, "I dessay the undertakers'll be coming along soon. You see them and make plans for the funeral; while Bill and I go on over this house. Then, we'll have to see the rest of the people who were around at the time of the—the tragedy."

"Not Mrs. Frederick Varian," said Herbert, "you can't see her. I forbid that, as her physician."

"Well, we'll see your wife first, and then, we'll have to see the folks that went back to the village. And there's the servants to be questioned."

But the careful and exhaustive search of the two inquiry agents failed to disclose any sign of the missing Betty Varian or any clue to her whereabouts. They went over the whole house, even into the bedroom of the newly made widow,—whose deep artificial sleep made this possible.

This was the last room they visited, and as they tiptoed out, Bill said,

"Never saw such a case! No clue anywhere; not even mysterious circumstances. Everything just as natural and commonplace as it can be."

"There's the yellow pillow,—" suggested Potter.

"I know,—but that may have some simple explanation,—housemaid took it out to clean it,—or something."

"Then, Bill, there's got to be a secret passage; there's just got to."

"Well, there ain't. Tomorrow, I'll sound the walls and all that sort of thing, but I've measured and estimated, and I vow there ain't no space unaccounted for in this whole house. But there's a lot of questionin' yet to be done. I'll say there is!"

By this time some of the servants had heard of the affair and had returned.

Potter and Bill Dunn went to the kitchen to see them, and found Kelly the butler and Hannah the cook in a scared, nervous state.

"Do tell us, sir, all about it," Kelly begged, his hard face drawn with sympathy. "The master—"

"It's true, Kelly, your master is dead. He was killed, and we are investigating. What can you tell us? Do you know of anybody who had it in for Mr. Varian?"

"Oh, no, sir! I'm sure he hadn't an enemy in the world."

"Oh, no, you can't be sure of that, my man. But tell me of the circumstances. When you all went away, this afternoon, there was no sign of disturbance,—of anything unusual?"

"Oh, no, sir. Everything was pleasant and proper. I had packed the luncheon for the picnic, Hannah here made the sandwiches, and I filled the coffee Thermos, and all such things. The baskets were all ready, and the family expected to start on the picnic almost as soon as we went off. I offered to stay behind and help Mrs.

Varian, but she was so kind as to say I needn't do that. So we all went."

"All at once?"

"Yes, sir."

"You went down the path that leads from the front door?"

"There's no other way. It branches around to the kitchen entrance, up here, but there's no other way off the premises."

"Not even for a burglar or robber?"

"No, sir. I don't believe even a monkey could scramble up the cliff, and I know a man couldn't. You see it overhangs, and it's impossible."

"But coming from the other direction,—the village?"

"From that way, everybody has to pass through the lodge gate. The lodge, you know,—that's the garage, as well. There's a gate here—"

"Yes, I know."

"Well, through that gate is the only way to get to this house."

"But all the picnic party were waiting, in full view of that gate, and in full view of the house. Yet somebody "

"You needn't say somebody got in,—for nobody could do that."

"I don't say it. But I'm looking out for some such person. If not, we must conclude—"

"What, sir?"

"That Miss Varian shot her father, and then,—in some yet undiscovered place, killed herself, or still alive,—is in hiding."

"Miss Betty kill her father!" exclaimed Hannah, the cook, speaking to the sheriff for the first time. "No, she never did that!"

"Yet there was ill feeling between them," Potter returned, quickly.

"That there was not! A more loving father and child I never met up with! Bless her pretty face! To dare accuse darlin' Miss Betty of such a thing! I say, now, Mister

Man, you better be careful how you say such lies around here! You know you've nothin' to go on, but your own black thoughts! You know you don't know who killed the master, and you're too dumb to find out, and so you pick on that poor dear angel child, who ain't here to speak up for herself!"

"Where is she, then? Where's Miss Betty?"

"Where is she? Belike in some hidin' place, scared into fits because of seein' her father shot! Or maybe, stunned and unconscious herself,—the deed bein' done by the same villyun what did for the master! Oh, sakes! it's bad enough without your makin' it worse callin' my darlin' girl a murderer! Where's Mrs. Varian? What does she say?"

"She's asleep. The doctor had to quiet her, she was in raving hysterics."

"Ay, she would be. Poor lady. She'll be no help in this awful thing. And, sir, another thing: The waitress and the chambermaid, they're sisters, Agnes and Lena, they say they're not coming back here. Nothing would induce them to step foot in this house again, they say. They bid me send 'em their things and—"

"Nonsense, they'll have to come back." This from Bill. "Tell me where they are. I'll bring them back."

"No, they won't come. They're going down to Boston tonight."

"They mustn't be allowed to do that!"

"They've gone by now," and Hannah looked unconcerned. "But never you mind, they know nothin' of this matter. They're two young scared girls, and they'd be no good to you nor anyone else. They know nothin' to tell, and they'd have worse hysterics than Mrs. Varian if you tried to bring 'em back to this house."

"You won't desert Mrs. Varian, will you, Hannah?" asked Potter.

"Well, I'll be leavin' in the mornin'," and the cook shrugged her shoulders. "I couldn't be expected to stay in such a moil."

"No; of course you couldn't!" exclaimed Potter, angrily. "You don't care that poor Mrs. Varian is in deep trouble and sorrow! You don't care that there'll be nobody to cook for her and her brother's family! You've no sense of common humanity,— no sympathy for grief, no heart in your stupid old body!"

"I might stay on for a time, sir,—if—if they made it worth my while."

"Oh, greed might keep you here! Kelly, what about you? Are you going to desert this stricken household?"

"I'll—I'll stay for a time, sir," the butler said, quite evidently ill at ease. "Now, you mustn't blame us, Mr. Potter for—"

"I do blame you! I know how you feel about a house where there's a mystery, but also, you ought to be glad to do whatever you can to help. And nothing could help poor Mrs. Varian so much as to have some of her servants faithful to her. Also, I'm pretty sure I may promise you extra pay,—as I know that will hold you, when nothing else will."

"And now," Bill Dunn put in, you'd better fix up a meal for those who want it. They had no picnic supper, you see, and there are the guests to be considered as well as your Mrs. Varian."

"Speakin" one word for them and two for yourself, I'm thinkin'," Hannah sniffed, as she began to tie on her apron. "Well, Mr. Potter, you'll be welcome to a good meal, I'm sure."

"One moment, Hannah," said Bill, "when you left here today, was there a sofa pillow out here in the kitchen?"

"A sofy pillow? There was not. Why should such a thing be?"

"A yellow satin one,—embroidered."

"Off the hall sofy? No, sir, it never was in my kitchen at all."

"What do you know about it?" Dunn turned to the butler. "When did you last see the sofa pillows on the hall sofa?"

Kelly stared.

"I saw them this morning, sir,—yes, and I saw them this afternoon,—when I set the picnic baskets out. I didn't—"

"How did you happen to notice the pillows, Kelly?" Bill watched him closely.

"Why, I didn't exactly notice them,—but,—well, if they hadn't been in place I should have noticed it."

"That's right," Dunn gave a satisfied nod. The pillow episode seemed important to him, though he could get no meaning to it as yet. Now Kelly, tell me the truth. When you've been around, in the dining room, or the living rooms, haven't you heard conversations between Miss Varian and her father that showed some friction between the two?"

"Oh, now, sir, Miss Betty's a saucy piece—"

"I don't mean gay chaff,—I mean real, downright quarreling. Did you ever hear any of that? Tell me the truth, Kelly, you'll serve no good purpose by trying to shield either of them."

"Well, then, yes, sir, I did,—and often. But not to say exactly quarreling,—more like argufying—"

"Why do you say that, Kelly? They do quarrel, —all the time they quarrel,—and you know it."

This astonishing speech was from the lips of Minna Varian, who suddenly appeared in the kitchen doorway.

She was smiling a little, she looked tired and wan, but she was in no way excited or hysterical. She wore a trailing blue wrapper, and her hair was falling from its combs and hairpins.

"Mrs Varian!" exclaimed Potter, springing to her side. "Why are you here?"

"I heard voices and I wondered who was down here. Where are my people? Who are you two strange men?"

"There, there," said Hannah, advancing and putting an arm round her mistress, "let me take you back to your room. Come now."

"Just a minute," and Potter looked keenly at the lady. "Say that again, Mrs. Varian. Your daughter quarrels with her father often?"

"All the time," Minna Varian laughed. "I have to make peace between them morning, noon and night. Oh, why do they do it? Fred is so dear and sweet to me,—then he will scold Betty for the least trifle! And Betty never differs from me in her opinions, but she is antagonistic to her father, always. Can you explain it?"

Mrs Varian's large gray eyes stared at Potter, and then turned to Bill Dunn. It was clear to be seen that she was still partly under the influence of the opiate effects, and that her memory of the recent tragedy was utterly obliterated.

"Take her to her room," Potter said quickly, to Hannah. "If she comes to down here there'll be a fearful scene. How did she get away?"

"There was nobody in my room," Minna said, overhearing. "Who should be there? I'm not ill. I woke up from a nap, and I heard talking,—my room is right above this, so I came down. Where's Miss Betty, Hannah? Kelly, what are you doing?"

"I'm about to get supper, madam," Kelly's glance rested kindly on the pathetic figure.

Minna Varian looked small and frail, and her white face and vacant, staring eyes seemed to add to the mystery of the whole affair.

"Come, now, Mrs. Varian, come along of Hannah."

"Minna, where are you?" Janet's frightened voice broke in upon them. "Merciful powers, however did she get down here? Help me get her back, Hannah. No, wait, I'll call Doctor Varian."

But Herbert Varian was already entering the kitchen, and between them, Minna was safely convoyed back to her room.

"Well, we're getting at the truth," said Potter, with an air of satisfaction as he glanced at Dunn. "Lord knows I'm sorry for that poor woman, but they say children and fools speak the truth, and so, though she isn't herself, mentally, she told the truth about Miss Varian and her father being enemies."

"Oh, she didn't," Hannah moaned, wiping her eyes on her apron. "I tell you it wasn't as bad as Mrs. Varian makes out."

"Yes, it was," said Kelly, slowly. "You've no way of knowing, Hannah, you're always in the kitchen. But I'm about the house all the time, and I hear lots of talk. And it's just as Mrs. Varian said: Miss Betty and her father never agree. They scrap at the least hint of a chance; and though sometimes they're terribly affectionate and loving, yet at other times, they quarrel like everything."

"That's enough, Kelly; now keep quiet about this. Even if Miss Varian and her father were not always friendly, it may not mean anything serious and it may make trouble for the young lady if such reports get out."

"You expect to find Miss Betty, then?"

"Find her? Of course. You say yourself there's only one way out of these premises. We know she didn't go out that way, so, she must be here. There must be places we haven't yet discovered, where she is hiding,—or—or has been concealed."

"It's a fearful situation!" broke out Dunn. "That girl may be gagged and bound—in' some secret closet—"

"You say there are none, Bill."

"I do say I don't see how there can be any, but, good lord, Potter, the girl must be somewhere,— dead or alive!"

An attractive supper, largely consisting of the delicacies intended for the picnic, and supplemented by some hot viands, was soon in readiness.

Hannah was deputed to sit beside Mrs. Varian, now sleeping again, and the others, including the detectives, gathered round the table.

"I'd like the sum of your findings, so far," Doctor Varian said, raising weary eyes to Potter's, face.

"Pretty slim, Doctor," the sheriff responded. "But, I want to say, right now, that I've got to do my duty as I see it. Much as I'd like to spare the feelings of you people and all that, I've got to forge ahead and discover anything I may."

"Of course you have, Mr. Potter. Don't think I'd put a straw in the way of truth or justice. But, granting that you may speak with all plainness, where do you come out?"

"Only to the inevitable conclusion that Miss Varian killed her father and then killed herself, and her body will yet be found."

"Now, Potter," Dunn said, slowly, "don't go too fast. That is one theory, to be sure, but it's only a theory. You've nothing to back it up,—there's no evidence—"

"There's negative evidence, Bill. Nobody else could get up here to do that shooting, or, if he did, he couldn't get away again. Say, for a minute, that some intruder might have been concealed in the house, say he shot Mr. Varian, how'd he get out of here without being seen, and how did he do for the girl?"

"That's all so," Bill said, doggedly, "but it ain't enough to prove,—or, even to indicate that Miss Varian did the shooting. Where'd she get a pistol?"

"Pshaw, that's a foolish question! If she had nerve and ingenuity enough to shoot, she had enough to provide the gun."

"Betty never did such things," said Janet Varian with spirit. "That girl did sometimes have words with her father,—that's a mere nothing,—my own daughter does that,—but Betty Varian is a loving, affectionate daughter, and she no more killed her father than I did!"

"Small use in asserting things you can't prove," said Potter, devoting himself to his supper. "Next thing for me to do 's to see those other people,—the ones that were here this afternoon."

"All right," said Doctor Varian, "but what do you hope to learn from them? They don't know as much as we do. I was first on the spot, young Landon, who's gone home, was here with me, and those others stayed down on the

path waiting for us. See them, by all means, but I doubt
their helpfulness. Now, aside from that, and granting you
get no new evidence, what's to be done?"

"I think," Potter said thoughtfully, "you'd better offer
a reward for any news of Miss Varian. It's not likely to
bring results,—but it ought to be done, I think."

CHAPTER 6: THE VARIAN PEARLS

WHEN Bill Dunn went up on the porch of Mrs. Blackwood's bungalow that evening, he found a group of neighbors there, and was not at all surprised that they were discussing the dreadful affair of Headland House.

Claire Blackwood greeted the caller courteously and asked him to go inside the house with her.

"Let us all go," said Rodney Granniss. "I want to learn all about this case, and we're entitled to know."

"Come on, everybody," Dunn invited, "I want to ask a lot of questions and who knows where I may get the best and most unexpected answers."

Granniss and Lawrence North, with Ted Landon and John Clark, who had been up on the Headland in the afternoon, were the men, and Mrs. Blackwood and her young guest, Eleanor Varian were the only women present.

Yet Dunn seemed well satisfied as he looked over the group.

"Fine," he said, "all the witnesses I wanted, and all here together."

"We didn't witness anything," offered John Clark, who was apparently by no means desirous of taking part in the colloquy. "And, as I've an engagement, can't you question me first, and let me go?"

"Sure I can," returned Dunn, whose easy manners were not at all curbed by the more formal attitude of those about him. "Just tell the story in your own way, son."

Clark resented the familiar speech, but said nothing to that effect.

"There's little to tell," he began; "I'd never been up to Headland House before, and of course I'd never before

met the Varians,—any of them. I went on Mrs.
Blackwood's invitation, and after meeting the family and
their guests on the veranda, we all started for a picnic.
We had reached a point half way down the steep path
from the house, when Miss Betty Varian said she had
forgotten her camera. She returned to the house for it,
and we waited. She was gone so long, that we
wondered,—and then, her father went to hurry her up.
He, too, was gone a long time, and then, Doctor Varian
and Ted Landon went after him. That's my story. Landon
can tell you the rest."

"I know the rest," said Dunn, shortly; "I don't see, Mr.
Clark, that you need remain. Your evidence is merely
that of all the party who stayed behind while the others
went up to the house."

"Yes," said Clark, with a sigh of relief, and making his
adieux, he went away.

"Have you formed any theory of the crime, Mr.
Dunn?" asked Lawrence North, who was consumed with
impatient curiosity, during the already known testimony
of Clark.

"Not a definite one," Dunn replied, seeming by his
manner to invite advice or discussion. "It is too
mysterious to theorize about."

"By Jove, it is!" North agreed; "I never heard of a case
so absolutely strange. I'd like to get into that house and
see for myself."

"See what for yourself Mr. North?"

"Whether there's any secret passage—but, of course
you've looked for that?"

"Yes; thoroughly. I'm of an architectural mind,—"

"So is Mr. North," said Mrs. Blackwood. "He designed
this bungalow we're in now."

"Are you an architect, Mr. North?"

"Not by profession, but I'm fond of it. And I flatter
myself I could discover a secret passage if such existed."

"I flatter myself I could, too," said Dunn, but not
boastfully. Yet, I may have overlooked it. I'd be obliged,

Mr. North, if you'd come up to the house, and give it the once over. You might spot what I failed to see."

"But I don't know the people at all—"

"No matter; I ask you as a matter of assistance. Come up there tomorrow, will you?"

North promised to do so, and Dunn turned to Eleanor Varian.

"Sorry to trouble you, Miss Varian, but I have to ask you some very definite questions. First, do you know your relatives up there pretty well?

"Why, yes," said Eleanor, with a surprised look. "They live in New York and we live in Boston, but we visit each other now and then and we often spend our summers at the same place. Of course, I know them well."

"Then, tell me exactly the relations between Miss Varian and her father. Don't quibble or gloss over the facts,—if they were not entirely in accord it will be found out, and you may as well tell the truth."

Eleanor Varian looked thoughtful.

"I will tell the truth," she said, "because I can see it's better to do so. Betty and her mother are much more in sympathy with one another than Betty and her father. I don't know what makes the difference, but Aunt Minna always seems to want everything the way Betty wants it, while Uncle Fred always wants just the opposite."

"Yet Miss Betty was fond of her father?"

"Oh, yes; they were devoted, really,—I think. Only, their natures were different."

"Was there any special subject on which they disagreed?"

"There has been of late," Eleanor admitted, though with evident reluctance. "Of course Betty is a great belle. Of course, she has and has had many admirers. Now, Uncle Fred seems always to be willing for Betty to have beaux and young man friends, but as soon as they become serious in their attentions, and want to marry Betty, then Uncle Fred shoos them off."

It was, as yet, impossible for Eleanor to speak of her uncle in the past tense. The girl had not at all realized this sudden death, and couldn't help thinking and speaking of him as still alive. Nor could she realize Betty's disappearance. She was somewhat in a daze, and also over excited by the awfulness of the situation. She talked rapidly, yet coherently, and Dunn secretly rejoiced at her agitation, knowing he would learn more than if she had been cool and collected.

"But that's not at all an unusual thing," put in North, who felt sorry for Eleanor and wanted to relieve her all he could from the grilling fire of Dunn's questions. "I find that the majority of fathers resent the advances of their daughters' suitors. Now, mothers are different,—they encourage a match that seems to them desirable. But a father can't realize his little girl is growing up."

"Well, Lawrence," exclaimed Claire Blackwood, "for a bachelor, you seem to know a lot about family matters!"

"I've lots of friends, and I can't help noticing these things. Isn't it true, Miss Varian?"

"Yes," Eleanor said, "to a degree, it is. I mean, in some instances. Any way, it's quite true of Uncle Fred and Betty. Aunt Minna would be delighted to have Betty engaged to some nice young man, but Uncle Fred flies in a fury at mere mention of such a thing."

"I can swear to that," said Rodney Granniss. "I've known the Varians for two years, and it's quite true. Mrs. Varian smiled on the attachment between Betty and myself, but Mr. Varian most certainly did not!"

"What!" exclaimed Dunn, "you one of Miss Betty Varian's suitors?"

"Even so," said Granniss, calmly. "I knew them in New York. I came up here to be near Betty. And now, Mr. Dunn, I want to say that I'm going to do all I can to solve the mystery of Mr. Varian's death, but even more especially am I going to try to find Betty herself. I haven't been up to Headland House yet, for it—well, it seems awful to go there now that Mr. Varian can't put me out!"

"Look here, young man," Dunn gazed at him curiously, "it doesn't seem to occur to you that you yourself may be said to have an interest in Mr. Varian's death!"

"Meaning that I shot him!" Grannis looked amused. "Well,—if you can tell me how I accomplished it—"

"But, my dear sir, somebody accomplished it—"

"And it might as well be me!" The only trouble with your theory Mr. Dunn is, that I didn't do it. Investigate all you like, you can't pin the crime on me."

"And, I suppose you didn't abduct Miss Betty either?"

"I did not!" Granniss looked solemn. "I only wish I had. But I'm going to find her, and I want to start out by being friendly with you, Mr. Dunn,—not antagonistic."

"Easy enough to check up your alibi, Mr. Granniss," Dunn said; "no, don't tell me where you were at the time,—I'll find out for myself."

"I'll tell you," said North, casually. "Mr Granniss was out in his motor boat all the afternoon. I know, because I was out in mine, and I saw him frequently. We were both fishing.

"That's right," said Granniss, carelessly, as if his alibi were of small moment to him, as indeed it was.

"Now, Mr. Dunn, you must have some theory,—or if not a theory, some possible explanation of what occurred. Do give it to us."

"Yes, do," said North. "I'm fond of detective stories, but I never read one that started out so mysteriously as this."

"I haven't any theory," Dunn looked at each in turn, his eyes roving round the room as he talked, "I can't say as I can even dope out how it *could* have happened. But here's what I work on,—motive. That's the thing to seek first,—motive. We know Mr. Varian is dead, we know Miss Varian is missing. That's all we really know. Now, you can't deduce anything from those facts alone. So, I say, hunt for a motive. It isn't likely that Mr. Varian had any enemies up here. And if he had, they never'd chosen such an opportunity to shoot him,—for, just think how sudden, how unexpected that opportunity was! Who could have foreseen that Miss Varian would go back to the house for her camera? Who could have foreseen that her father would go back after her? If those goings back were unpremeditated, then no enemy could have been there ready to utilize his chance. If, on the other hand, those goings back were premeditated, then they were arranged by either Miss Betty or her father "

"Impossible!" cried North. "Mr Varian couldn't foresee that his daughter would forget her camera, and Miss Betty couldn't foresee that it would be her father who would come back for her!"

"I know it seems that way," Dunn looked deeply perplexed, "but I can't get away from the idea of there being some premeditation about the two goings back to that empty house that resulted in a double tragedy."

"Suppose a burglar—" began Claire Blackwood; "suppose he had been concealed in the house before we left to go to the picnic. Suppose when Betty came back unexpectedly, he attacked her, and then, when Mr. Varian came—"

"But what became of the burglar,—and of Miss Betty?" asked Dunn. "I've mulled over the burglar proposition, I've imagined him to be one of the servants, but it all comes back to the fact that such an intruder just simply couldn't get away, and couldn't get Betty away, dead or alive."

"That's perfectly true," Claire agreed. "There's no way to dispose of an imaginary intruder. But neither is there any way to dispose of Betty. Nothing in this world will make me believe that girl shot her father, but just assuming, for a moment, that she did,—what happened next?"

Claire demanded this with the air of an accusing judge.

"Why, that's the only possible theory," said Dunn. "Say the young lady did shoot her father, then she went some place,—where, we haven't yet discovered, —and shot herself,—or, is there, alive yet."

"If that's the case, I'll find her!" Rodney Granniss burst forth, his strong young face alight with zeal; "I'm going up there at once. Mr. Varian didn't like me, but Mrs. Varian does, and maybe I can help her."

"She can't see you," Dunn told him. "She's under the influence of opiates all the time. Doctor Varian keeps her that way."

"She'll have to come to her senses some time," said Rod. "I'm going up there any way."

"I'm going with you," declared Eleanor Varian. "I don't want to stay here,—forgive me, Mrs. Blackwood, you're kindness itself,—but I want to be where father and mother are. I want to help find Betty, too. I know a lot of places to look—"

"You do!" exclaimed Dunn. "Where are they, now?"

But all that Eleanor mentioned, Dunn had already searched, and his hopes of the girl's assistance fell. Still, she might be familiar with Betty's ways, and might be of some slight use.

"Well, Miss Varian, you must do as you think best," he said; "but I advise you to bide here till the morning, anyway."

"Yes, do, dear," urged Claire, and Eleanor, remembering the unavoidable climb up the steep rocks, consented.

"Tell me one thing, Miss Varian," said Dunn, suddenly; "were you in the kitchen of the Varian house this afternoon at all?"

"Yes, I was; I went out there with Betty to get some cakes and things. Why?"

"When you were there, did you notice a yellow sofa pillow out there?"

"In the kitchen? No, I did not!"

"You know the two yellow cushions that belong on the hall sofa?"

"Yes,—I think I know the ones you mean. What about them?"

"We found one of them in the middle of the kitchen floor. Do you think anybody could have put it there purposely?"

"I can't imagine why any one should!"

"What do you deduce from that?" Lawrence North asked, interestedly, and Claire said:

"Why, that's what you call a clue, isn't it? What does it show?"

"It doesn't show a thing to me," declared Dunn; "leastways, nothing sensible. Look here, folks,— either there was somebody else in that house at that time besides Betty and her father,—or else there wasn't. Now if there was, he surely wouldn't be moving sofa pillows about. And if there wasn't, then one of those two people moved it. Now, why? I can't think of any reason, sensible or not, that would make anybody lug a fine handsome sofa cushion out to the kitchen."

"Was it valuable enough to be worth stealing?" asked North.

"No; a good looking affair, but nothing to tempt a thief."

"Looks like the servants' work, I think," suggested Claire. "Suppose one of them had stayed behind, and not with any criminal intent, either; and suppose, merely to be luxurious, she had taken a fine pillow out to her kitchen quarters."

"But even so, and even if she were caught by the returning Betty she couldn't have shot Mr. Varian and concealed both herself and Betty—"

"You run up against a stone fence whatever you surmise," exclaimed Landon. He had been a quiet listener, but had done some deep thinking. "There's only one plausible solution,—and that's a secret passage."

"Look here, Mr. Landon," Dunn said, sharply, "that speech gets on my nerves. Anybody who thinks there's a secret passage in that house up there on the cliff is welcome to go up there and find it. But I'm no fool and sheriff Potter isn't either; nor is Doctor Herbert Varian. And none of us can find a secret passage, and what's more, we're positive there isn't any. So, either show where there could be one,—or let up on that solution."

"Good lord, Dunn, don't get so wrathy!" Landon said, good humoredly. "And I will go and look for one,—since you invite me. Go with me, North?"

"Yes," was the willing reply, and Rodney Granniss said:

"Well you fellows won't want to make that search till tomorrow. But I'm going up to the house now. You'll stay here, won't you, Miss Varian?"

Reluctantly, Eleanor agreed to stay, and Granniss went off alone.

Rodney Granniss was a determined man, and when he made his mind to hunt for Betty Varian he also made up his mind to find her. To his mind the very fact that the whole case was so inexplicable made it likely to develop some sudden clue or key that would unlock the situation.

He still felt averse to visiting a house where his presence had been forbidden by one who was now unable to resent his coming, but this was offset by his desire to help Mrs. Varian and to help in finding Betty.

He pondered over the idea of a secret passage in the house, but it was of small comfort to him. If those other indefatigable workers had not been able to find it, he had no reason to think he could do so. And, besides, it was anything but an attractive picture to imagine Betty, either hidden voluntarily or concealed against her will in some such place.

He trudged along up the rocky steps and presented himself at the door of Headland House.

Sheriff Potter admitted him, and listened to his story.

Then he took him to the library and introduced him to Doctor Varian and his wife.

"I am glad to see you," cried Janet. "Tell me of Eleanor."

"She's all right," returned Granniss, cheerfully. She rather wanted to come up here with me, but they persuaded her to stay over night with Mrs. Blackwood."

"Better so," said Doctor Varian. "Did Dunn learn anything from anybody that you know of?"

"No," said Rodney, "and I fear there's little to learn from anybody."

"Meaning?"

"Meaning that whatever there is to be learned must be found out here in this house,—not from any of those onlookers."

"Sensible talk," said Doctor Varian, "but how shall we set about it?"

"I don't know. I'm not possessed of what is called detective instinct, nor am I especially clever at solving puzzles. But I have determination, and I'm going to devote my whole time and energy to finding Betty Varian!"

"Well said, young man," put in Potter, who was listening, "but untrained sleuthing is not often productive of great results."

"I don't mean sleuthing, exactly," and Granniss looked at him squarely, "I am untrained. But I'm willing to be advised, I'm willing to be dictated to; I only ask to help."

"You're a brick!" said Janet; "I shouldn't be surprised if you succeed better than the detectives."

"If so, it will be because of my more personal interest in the case. I ought to tell you, Mrs. Varian, that Betty and I are practically engaged. It depended, of course, on her father's consent—"

"And that he refused to give?" asked Potter.

"Yes, he did. Which immediately ticketed me as his murderer in the eyes of Mr. Dunn. But I'm not a criminal, and I didn't shoot Mr. Varian. I shan't insist on this point, because you can prove my words true for yourself. Now, I'd like a talk with Mrs. Varian,—Betty's mother,—when such a thing is possible—and convenient."

"I'm not sure but it would be a good thing," said Doctor Varian, thoughtfully; "when she wakes, Mr. Granniss, she will either be hysterical still, and in need of further opiate treatment, or,—and which I think more likely,—she will be calm, composed and alert minded. In the latter case, she might be glad to talk to the man who cares so much for her daughter."

"I hope so; and, in the mean time, what can we do in the matter of finding Betty?"

"There's nothing to be done in that line that hasn't been done," said the sheriff, despairingly.

"All evening Doctor and Mrs. Varian as well as the butler and cook have been going over the house and the grounds, calling, and hunting for the girl, with no success of any sort."

"Had she a dog?"

"No, there is none about. Now, just before you came, we were thinking of looking over some of Mr. Frederick Varian's papers—"

"And there's no reason to change our plans," said Doctor Varian; "Mr Granniss' presence will not interfere."

So Rodney sat by, awaiting the possible awakening of Mrs. Varian, and trying hard to think of some new way to look for Betty.

With keys obtained from the pockets of the dead man, his brother opened the drawers of the desk.

"It must be done," he said, as his hand slightly hesitated, "and, too, we may come across some clue to his death."

Among the first of the important papers found was Frederick Varian's will. The contents of this were a surprise to no one present, for the entire estate was left to the wife, with instructions that she make due and proper provisions for the daughter. But a final clause caused Herbert Varian to stare incredulously at the paper.

"What is it, dear?" Janet asked, seeing his astonishment.

"Why,—why, Janet! the Varian pearls are left to Eleanor!"

"To Eleanor? No!"

"But they are! See, it's plain as day!"

There was no doubt as to his statement. The final clause of Frederick Varian's last will and testament, bequeathed the string of pearls, known as 'the Varian pearls,' to his niece, Eleanor, the daughter of his brother Herbert.

"Just what is so startling in that?" asked Potter, curiously, and Doctor Varian replied:

"The Varian pearls are an heirloom, and are valued at two hundred thousand dollars. It is the custom for the oldest of the family to inherit them, and he is expected to bequeath them to his oldest child. Why did my brother leave them to my daughter instead of to Betty?"

"Herbert, it's dreadful! Eleanor shall not take them!" Janet cried.

"That makes no difference, ma'am," Potter said; "it's the fact that Mr. Varian left them away from his own child, that proves the attitude of the father to the daughter!"

CHAPTER 7: MINNA VARIAN

IT was not until after the funeral of her husband that Minna Varian really came to herself. The three intervening days, she had been free from hysterics but had been in a state of physical exhaustion and incapable of any exertion.

But on the day after the funeral, she seemed to take on a new vitality.

"I have come to life," she said, speaking very seriously. "I have at last realized what has happened to me. I was dazed at first, and couldn't seem to get my senses. Now, we will have no more hysterics, no more emotional scenes, but we go to work to find my child,—to save what I can from my wrecked life. It is a wonder that I didn't lose my mind utterly. Think of it, Herbert, to lose my husband by death and my child by a mystery far worse than death—"

Minna showed signs of breaking down again, but forced herself to control her voice.

"I have made up my mind," she went on, "to go about the search for Betty systematically and immediately. The detectives can do nothing,—they have proved that. The sheriff and that Mr. Dunn are at the end of their rope. I don't blame them,— it is a baffling case. And I know they think Betty's dead body is hidden somewhere on the premises. Though how they can think that, I don't see, after the search that has been made."

"They think it," Janet said, "because there's no other possible conclusion. You know, yourself, Minna, if Betty were alive we would know of it by this time."

"Never mind theories or conclusions," Minna said, determinedly, "action is what I want. I know my Betty never killed her father! I know that as well as I know that

I'm alive. And Betty may be dead or alive,—but I'm going to find her in any case. Now, first of all, I suppose you people want to get away from here. Herbert, your practice is calling you, of course. I'm not going to keep you. But I'm going to stay here, on these premises, where my child disappeared, until I get some knowledge of what happened to her."

"But, Minna," Varian objected, "you can't stay here alone—"

"Then I'll get some one to stay with me. I can get a companion or a nurse or a secretary,—you see, Herbert, there's a lot of business to be attended to in connection with Fred's papers and affairs. He left me very well off, but the financial settling up will call for the trained work of a good lawyer or accountant."

"Young Granniss spoke to me about that," Doctor Varian said; "he's a bright young lawyer, you know, and he thought perhaps you'd employ him, and then he thought he'd help you in the search for Betty."

"I'd like that. Rod's a nice chap, and truly, Fred had nothing against him, except that he wanted to take Betty away from us. It would be no slighting of Fred's wishes if I should have to do with Mr. Granniss,—and nobody could be better help to me in my search."

"I can't see, Minna," said Janet, "what you hope from that search. Every nook and cranny of this whole place has been thoroughly examined, and as nothing has been found "

"That's just it, Janet," Minna spoke patiently, "because nothing has been found is the very reason I must search more and further. I shall, first of all, offer a large reward. The size of the reward may bring information when no other means would."

"Make the offer as large as you like, Minna," Varian said, but not unkindly, "for you'll never be called upon to pay it. Why, child, there's no hope. I don't want to be brutal, but really, Minna, dear, you oughtn't to buoy yourself up with these false hopes, that never can be realized."

"Look here, Herbert, what do you think happened to my child? Who do you think killed Fred?"

"Since you ask me, Minna, I must say, in all honesty, that I can't see any possible theory or any imaginable explanation except that Betty shot her father, and then shot herself."

"Where is she, then?"

"Hidden in some secret cupboard in this house. that she knew of, but that we haven't yet found."

"I can see, Herbert," Minna spoke slowly, "how you can believe that, because, as you say, you can't think of any other case. But I know,—I know Betty never shot her father. I know that,—and I shall yet prove it."

"But, Minna, there must have been more enmity between Fred and Betty than you know of, to make him leave the Varian pearls to Eleanor."

"That is incredible," Minna mused. "I can't understand that and I shouldn't believe it, if it were not right there in Fred's own handwriting. I haven't seen the pearls for some years. I've been too much of an invalid to wear them often, and they've stayed in the safe deposit for the last five or six years. But I meant Betty should wear them next winter. Of course, I was sure Fred would leave them to her in his will. I can't understand it! It isn't so much the loss of the value that affects me, as the appalling fact that he wanted to leave them away from Betty. As you say, there must have been something between those two,—something desperate that I don't know about."

"But what could there be?" Janet said, a blank wonder on her face.

"That's the very point," said Minna. "I know there has never been any special or particular ground for disagreement between those two except as to the matter of Betty's getting married,—or engaged. Fred never would consent to that. But of course he would have done so, later. He didn't approve of very early marriages,—but more, I think, he dreaded the idea of Betty's going away from us."

"Yet that only proves a special and even selfish fatherly love," Varian said, "and in that case, why take the pearls away from her?"

"I can't understand it," said Minna again; "it is too amazing! He adored Betty, and what ever possessed him to give the pearls to Eleanor,—he liked Eleanor, as we all do, but he never seemed especially attached to her. Not to put her ahead of Betty, anyway!"

"Of course she shall never take the pearls," said Janet, decidedly. "I think Fred was temporarily out of his mind when he made that will, or he was temporarily angry at Betty. When is it dated?"

"That's the strange part," said Minna. "He made that will ten years ago."

"When Betty was only about ten years old! He couldn't have been angry at the child then!"

"I think that is the only explanation," Doctor Varian said. "I can't think of any other explanation except that Fred was foolishly angry at the child, and in a fit of silly temper made the will giving the pearls to Eleanor, and then forgot all about it."

"Forgot the Varian pearls!" cried Janet; "not likely. But I never shall let Eleanor accept them."

"Don't say that, my dear," remonstrated her husband. "If Betty never is found, of course it's right Eleanor should have the pearls. I am the next Varian to Fred, and my daughter is the rightful heir,—after Betty."

"That's true," said Minna. "But let that matter rest for the present. If Betty is never found, Eleanor ought to have the pearls. If Betty is found, I shall be so happy, I don't care what becomes of them!"

"You're right, Minna," Doctor Varian said, "in thinking I ought to get back to the city. But Janet or Nell or both will stay here with you as long as you need or want them."

"Only till I can get somebody else. I've about concluded to take Rodney Granniss as secretary and have him settle up Fred's estate. With the cooperation of Fred's own lawyers. Then, I'll have a sort of nurse companion who can look after me, and then, I shall devote my life and, if need be, all my money to solving my mysteries. I shall get the best detectives in the country. I shall follow out also some ideas of my own, and if success is possible, I shall attain it."

Minna sat upright, her eyes shining with a clear, steady determined light. She seemed another being from the one who had screamed in hysterics at first knowledge of her sorrows.

"I've found myself," she said, in explanation. "I've risen above my dead self of grief and sorrow. Why, my desolation is so great, so unspeakable, that I must do something or go mad! I'm not mad,—I have too much to do. Now, Janet, if you and Eleanor,—or one of you, will stay a day or two longer, I'll get a nurse up from the city, and as soon as she arrives you can go. I know you'll be glad to get away from this place of horrors—"

"Not that, Minna, dear, but we have several engagements—"

"Yes, of course, I know. Well, plan for two days more,—I'll be settled by that time."

And she was. Inside of forty eight hours, the now energetic woman had Rodney Granniss installed as her secretary and man of business, and had secured the services of a capable and kindly woman as nurse and companion. Her new household made up, she let her relatives go back to their own summer home, and devoted herself to her life work.

"Of course," she said to Granniss, "we must go ahead on the supposition that Betty is alive."

"And she is, Mrs. Varian," the young man said, earnestly. "For, North and I have been all over this place, and North is a sort of an architect, you know, and I'm sort of a detective, and we can't find any place where any one could be concealed. Now, it doesn't do any good, as some do, to say there must be a secret passage, or secret cupboard. If there were, we must have found it. And it's too ridiculous, even to think for a minute that Betty killed her father! I know Betty, even better, perhaps than you or her father ever knew her. We have been sweethearts for nearly a year, and I tried many a time to persuade Betty to defy her father, and announce her engagement to me. She would have done so soon, I'm sure, but it was her love and respect for him that made her hold off so long. As to their little squabbles, they meant nothing at all. To imagine that girl shooting anybody is too absurd! I could rather imagine—"

Granniss paused, and Minna took up his thought.

"You could rather imagine her father shooting her! I've thought that over, but you see, it's impossible, because there was no weapon found."

"It's the strangest case I ever heard of! Now, about the reward. It's time that was attended to."

"Yes; and I think we'll make it as high as ten thousand dollars,—"

"For Betty's return?"

"Yes, that is, for any information that may lead to knowledge of what happened to Betty and where she is now."

"Nothing about apprehending the criminal?"

"You know, Mr. Granniss, they make fun of me for imagining this 'criminal.' How could there be one? How did he get in the house? How did he disappear again? You say yourself there's no secret passage,—we know nobody came in through the regular way,—how, then, even suggest a 'criminal'?"

"Yes, but why offer a reward, if there's no one who could by any chance appear to claim it?"

"That's the point Doctor Varian makes. He says it doesn't matter how large we make the offer, for it never will be claimed."

"Then we'll just assume that criminal, and go ahead with the reward plan," said Granniss, cheerfully. "I'll attend to it, and we won't speculate on its result at present. It surely can't do any harm. But, Mrs. Varian, we must do more than that."

"What, for instance?"

"Detectives. I think you should get the best one you can and get him up here at once."

"Please do that, Mr. Granniss. What do you do? Apply to a city agency?"

"Yes; or get a private detective. I know of one, —the best there is in the country, but we might not be able to get him."

"Try, anyway. Offer any price,—any bonus. Only get him."

"Very well,—I'll try. I have to go down to New York soon, for there are many important matters to see to with Mr. Varian's lawyers. I'll see about this detective then."

Minna had replaced the servants who had left her with maids from the village. There were some who were glad to go to a house suddenly made famous by such an astounding mystery. Others declared the house was haunted, and wouldn't go near it.

Among those who inclined to the haunted house idea was the new nurse. A Mrs. Fletcher: she was of a psychic turn of mind, and while she didn't exactly believe Betty was carried off by spooks, yet she thought the girl might have taken her own life, and perhaps her father's, because of supernatural influences or directions.

"Rubbish'" Minna Varian told her. "My Betty was,— is,—a healthy, normal girl. She has none of those foolish notions of the occult or supernatural."

"It's the only explanation," said Mrs. Fletcher, doggedly. "And I do think the house is haunted,—I heard mysterious sounds last night,—like rustling of wings."

Minna Varian only looked amused at this, but Granniss, who was present, said, "That's interesting, Mrs. Fletcher. Tell me about it. The account, however, was merely a vague idea of sounds, that might have been mysterious, but were more likely made by the servants going about at night.

Sheriff Potter and his colleague, Bill Dunn, had practically given up the matter. They pretended to be working on it, but as they themselves put it, "What can you do when you can't do nothin'?"

There was room for much discussion, but when it came to action, what was there to be done?

You can't hunt a criminal when you've no reason to assume any criminal intent. You can't hunt for a missing girl after you've scoured all the places where she could by any possibility be found. You can't hunt for the murderer of a man when there was no way for a murderer to be on the scene.

"Then are you going to give up the quest?" Granniss asked of the sheriff.

"No, not that," Potter said, uneasily. "We're open to suggestion,—we're keen for any new clue or testimony,—but where can we look for such? You must see, Mr. Granniss, that it's a mighty unusual case,—a most mysterious and unsolvable case."

"I do see that, and that's why I'm going to get expert assistance."

"Go ahead," said Potter, agreeably. "I'll be glad to see any man who can handle the thing. Why, there's no handle to it. No place to catch hold. Here's a man killed, and a girl missing. Now, we've no more idea what happened to those two people than we had at the moment of the discovery of the situation."

"That's perfectly true."

"And what's more, we never will have. That mystery will never be solved."

"You're saying that, Mr. Potter, doesn't necessarily make it true."

"No; but it's true all the same. If Miss Betty was in any way to blame,—which, I can't believe,—you'll never find out anything. Because, if she's alive she'd have shown up by this time."

"Go on,—and if Miss Betty was not to blame—"

"Then, whoever was to blame made a blame good job of it,—and you'll never catch him!"

"That's the principle I'm going to work on,—the idea that somebody did do it,—that he did make a good job of it,—and that I am going to catch him!"

"Fine talk, but there's the same old stumbling block. You can't argue an outsider,—an intruder, without allowing a secret entrance to that house,— and you say there isn't any."

"There sure isn't."

"Well, suppose your criminal didn't arrive and depart in an aeroplane?"

"I've thought of that,—but it isn't possible. You see there were half a dozen people looking on all the time. I wish I'd been there!"

" 'Twouldn't have done any good. You couldn't 'a' seen more'n anybody else did. There was nothing to see."

"No," agreed Granniss, "there was nothing to be seen."

Lawrence North came up to the house again at Rod's request, and once more they looked for a secret room or cupboard.

Armed with a yardstick and measuring tape, they went through the house from roof to cellar. They paced floors and measured walls and tapped ceilings, and proved to their own conviction that there was no foot of space in the whole structure unaccounted for.

"It isn't," said North, "as if it were an old English manor house or a medieval castle. It's modern, it isn't built with any sinister plan or any desire for secret maneuvers. There never was any smuggling going on up as far as this, and, anyway, this is a simple pleasure house, built for a pleasant simple family life. I've looked up the builders, and they say it was built by a commonplace man with a commonplace family. They moved out of the state long ago, but there never was anything secretive or mysterious about them."

They spent a long time in the cellar, but here, too, there was no uncertain space. Everything was built four square. Every room, bin or cupboard was as plainly defined as those above, and there was no hiding place possible.

Granniss looked down the old dried up well.

"Dunn went down that," Lawrence said; "nothing doing."

"I've got to go down myself," returned Rodney, shortly, as he took off his coat.

"Be careful, then," North admonished him. "I'll hold the light."

A good, strong flashlight illuminated the old well, and Rod Granniss clambered down its stone sides. But he returned with the same message Dunn had brought.

"All dried up; nothing down there but a muddy bottom and moss grown stones."

"No stones missing?"

"No; all solid and complete. I gave it a most careful scrutiny, for I don't want to have to go down again."

"Well, that finishes the cellar, then."

"Yes; and finishes the house. You must admit, Lawrence, there's no possible chance of Betty Varian being in this house, dead or alive."

"Of course, I admit that,—but, what, then?"

"I can't even suggest! Can you?"

"There's nothing left but that she went away,— managed somehow to elude the watchers,—perhaps they were not noticing the house."

"You talk as if she could get down from this headland by any other route than right past where the crowd were waiting."

"Maybe she hid here in the house, until after dark "

"Oh, don't suggest such awful things! Betty kill her father, and then, hiding until dark, make her way out and down to the village and away from the Harbor—oh, impossible!"

"Alternative?"

"I don't know! The more I think it over the less I can see any solution!"

"What about the haunted house idea?"

"That doesn't mean a thing to me," Granniss scorned it. "In fact, I usually come back to the idea that Mr. Varian in some way killed himself."

"Weapon?"

"I know, but I mean, maybe he shot himself, and Betty, who might have been trying to prevent it, took the pistol and ran away."

"Why?"

"Oh, I don't *know!* You are too exasperating, Lawrence! You just stand there and say 'why'? Stop it."

"Keep your temper, Rod. I'm only trying, as you are, to find some way to look. It is indeed impenetrable!"

"And then that matter of the pearls."

"To me that is the strangest revelation yet. No matter how much the father and daughter had little disagreements, even quarrels, how could he leave that great treasure away from his child and give it to his niece!"

"I think that very thing is a key to the mystery."

"How do you mean?"

"I don't know. You know I don't know, Lawrence; if I did I'd have told long ago! But I believe when the worthwhile detective that I'm going to get for Mrs. Varian takes hold of the case, he'll work from that strange bequest of the Varian pearls."

"Maybe he will,—but to me,—while it's passing strange, it doesn't seem to indicate anything definite."

"No, nor to me. But we haven't the trained mind of the real detective."

"Who's the man you're going to get?"

"Pennington Wise, the best in the country."

"I've heard of him. Well, it will be interesting to see how he goes about it."

CHAPTER 8: RANSOM

THE Herbert Varians went back to their summer home, and Minna, left alone with her companion and her secretary, began what she called her campaign to find Betty.

Some people thought Mrs. Varian a little affected mentally by her awful griefs, but those who knew her best read in her determination and persistence a steady aim and felt a slight hope of her success.

"Anything in the world I can do, dear," Claire Blackwood said to her, "command me. Ill go to the city for you or do errands or anything I can."

"No," said Minna, "there's nothing you can do. Nothing anybody can do. I'm only afraid that if I get no encouragement in my efforts, I will lose my mind,—and that's what I'm trying to guard against. I follow my nurse's directions as to exercise, diet and all that, but I feel as if I could only keep my brain from flying to pieces by hanging onto my hope of eventually finding my child."

"And you will," Claire said, earnestly, though she voiced a belief that she was far from feeling, "Oh, Mrs. Varian, you will!"

"You see," Minna went on, "I've a new theory now. I think that maybe Betty killed her father accidentally—"

"That is a new idea."

"Yes; I know it's almost incredible,—but what idea isn't? Say Mr. Varian went suddenly insane,—and I can't think of any other way,—and attacked Betty with a revolver. Say, trying to protect herself, it went off and killed him,—perhaps the weapon was in his hands, perhaps in hers,—and then, the child, in an agony of fear or remorse, ran away,—I don't know how she got away,—

but, don't you see, Mrs. Blackwood, she must have left the premises somehow,—or—"

"Or they would have found her by this time,—yes, of course."

"Now, I've offered ten thousand dollars reward for any information that will lead to finding Betty, —dead or alive. Mr. Granniss thinks it will bring no results, but I can't help hoping. And if it doesn't, —what can I do?"

"You're going to employ a detective, aren't you? These local authorities are not capable of managing a case like this."

"Yes; Mr. Granniss advises a Mr. Wise,—but I can't see what any detective can do. There's nothing to detect, as I can see."

"That's just it. We can't see,—but the trained detective can."

"Here is your mail, Mrs. Varian," said Granniss, coming into the room, "will you run it over?"

Minna glanced at the letters, mostly notes of sympathy, or letters of advice from would be helpful friends, but there was one that caused her to exclaim in amazement.

"Oh, Rodney," she cried, "will you look at this!" So great was her agitation that Claire Blackwood went in search of the nurse, for she feared some emotional outburst beyond her power to control.

The disturbing letter was a plain looking affair, on ordinary letter paper, and it read:

Mrs. Varian.
We have your daughter safe. We are holding her for ransom. Your reward does not tempt us at all but if you are ready to pay one hundred thousand dollars, you may have your child back. If not, you will never see her again. There must be no dickering, no fooling, and, above all, no police interference. I will not go into details now, but if you want to take up with this offer put a personal in any of the large Boston papers, saying, "I agree," and all

directions will be sent to you as to how to proceed. But if you tell the police or allow any detective to know anything about this deal, it is all off. Don't think you can fool us, we have eyes in the back of our heads and any insincerity or breach of faith on your part will result in sad results to your daughter. To carry this thing through you must trust and obey us implicitly and any lapse will mean far deeper trouble than you are in now."

The letter was not signed, nor was it dated. The postmark was Boston, and it had been mailed the day before.

"It's a fake," Granniss declared, at once.

"I don't think so," said Claire Blackwood, "it sounds real to me—"

"I don't care whether it's real or not," Minna interrupted, excitedly. "I mean I don't care whether anybody believes it's real or not. I'm going to answer it at once, and I'm going to agree to everything they say, and I'm not going to tell the police or a detective or anybody,—and I'm going to get Betty back."

Her face was radiant with joy, her eyes shone and she was smiling for the first time since that awful day of the double tragedy.

"Now, look here, Mrs. Varian," began Granniss, who was convinced the whole letter was a mere attempt to get money under false pretenses, "you mustn't throw away a hundred thousand dollars in that fashion!"

"Why not? It is a lot of money, but I have the sum and it means getting Betty back! What is any sum of money,—even my whole fortune, against that?"

"But it doesn't surely mean getting her back. If I thought it did I'd feel just as you do about it—"

"Oh, it does,—it does!" Minna cried, her face still transfigured with happiness. "I know it,—I feel it— something in my heart tells me that it is true,—and, you see, it explains everything. These people kidnapped Betty,—abducted her, and now they're holding her for

ransom,—and they'll get it,— and I'll get Betty! They
don't want her, you see, but they do want the money. And
they'll get it!"

"I agree with Mrs. Varian," Claire said, quite
convinced by Minna's confidence in the good faith of the
letter writer.

"But it's too absurd!" insisted Rodney. "You know,—
Mrs Varian, you must know, that I want to find Betty
quite as much as you do,—no, I won't qualify that
statement. I love her as much as you can. But I don't
believe for one minute that that letter is genuine. I mean,
I don't believe the man who wrote it has Betty, or ever
saw her! Why, think a minute. Of all the theories
regarding Betty's disappearance, abduction is the least
believable. How could any one abduct Betty that day,—
how could the kidnapper get into this house, and out
again,—with Betty,—when so many people were about,
watching?"

"I don't know how it was done," Minna said, doggedly,
"but it's a chance, and I'm going to take it. You can't stop
me, Rodney. You've no authority to say what I shall do
with my own money. I've a right to try this thing—"

"But, oh," said Claire, "suppose it should be a fake!
Not only you'd lose all that money,—but think of your
disappointment!"

"The disappointment would be no worse than things
are at present."

"Oh, yes, it would. If you follow up that letter and pay
all that sum, and then get nothing in return, it would just
about kill you."

"It would just about kill me not to take the chance,"
returned Minna. "Now, I suppose ,1 still have the right to
order my own movements. I shall at once send the
personal to the Boston paper,—I'll put it in several, so
he'll be sure to see it,—and then, I'll await his further
advice. Will you send the messages, Rodney, or must I do
it myself?"

"Of course, I am at your orders, Mrs. Varian." Rod gave her his winning smile, "But, at least, let's think it over a bit."

"No; send the word at once. We can talk it over afterward."

There seemed to be no way out, so Granniss went off to do her bidding.

Even then, he had half a mind to pretend to send the word but really to withhold it. On reflection, he concluded he had no right to do this. But he remembered that Minna had not bound him to secrecy, though, of course, it was implied.

So with the letters to the Boston papers went also one to Pennington Wise begging him to come at once to investigate the remarkable case of Betty Varian, and telling him frankly of the strange letter just received.

That same afternoon a telegram came for Mrs. Varian.

Granniss opened it, as was his custom, and its contents so surprised him that he nearly succumbed to the temptation to keep it from Mrs. Varian.

But, he reconsidered, he had no right to presume on his position as confidential secretary, so with grave fears of its effects he handed it to her.

"Dear Mother," it ran; *"I am all right, and if you do just as you agree, I will soon be with you again. Please obey implicitly.*

"BETTY."

"From her!" Minna cried, and fainted.

Nurse Fletcher soon revived her, but she was in a shaken, nervous state, and could stand no contradiction or disapproval.

"Now you see, Rodney," she cried triumphantly, "it is all right! Here is word from Betty herself—oh, my darling!" and she fell to kissing the yellow paper, as if it were the face of her child.

"But, Mrs. Varian," Granniss hesitated to correct her but felt he must, "that may not be from Betty, you know.

Anybody could send a telegram signed with Betty's name."

"Rodney!" Minna's eyes blazed with anger, "why do you try every way to make me miserable? Why dash every cup of joy from my lips? You seem to hope that we never find Betty! I can't understand your attitude, but unless you are more helpful,—yes, and more hopeful,—I don't think we can get along together."

But Granniss knew that he must stand by this distracted woman. Another secretary might have more leniency and less judgment, which would be a bad thing for Minna's interests. No, even at risk of letting her be imprudent, he must stand by her, and protect her all he could against her own wrong decisions.

"Oh, yes, we'll get along all right, Mrs. Varian," he said, trying to treat the matter lightly. "You can't get rid of me so easily,—and, too, you know that I want to believe all this quite as much as you do. But you must admit that a telegram is not like a letter. It might be faked."

"Well, this isn't," said Minna, contentedly, still caressing the paper missive.

"Let's consider it," said Rod. "It doesn't sound to me like Betty's diction. Would she use the word 'implicitly'?"

"Why not?" Minna stared at him. "And, too, she wrote it under compulsion, most likely. Oh, my darling child,— at the mercy of those ruffians! Yet, I make no doubt they're good to her. Why should they harm my baby? They, only want the ransom money, and that they shall have. I'm glad it's a large sum, it makes me more sure I'll get Betty."

Granniss was in despair. He felt the awful responsibility of Mrs. Varian's wild determination, but he couldn't see anything to do about it.

To report to Doctor Varian was not his duty, and though he thought it was his duty to tell the story to the police, Minna had exacted his promise not to do so, and he had given it. After all, it was her money,—if she chose to give it up so easily, it was not his affair. And, too, he couldn't help a lurking hope that it might be all true and might result in Betty's restoration to her sorrowing mother,—and, to himself. For he knew, now that the opposing influence of her father was removed, if Betty should ever be found, she would some day be his wife. He trusted in her faith and loyalty to himself as he believed in his own to her.

And yet, he couldn't approve of Minna's wholesale compliance with the exorbitant demands of people who might be and probably were mere swindlers. He was thinking these things over when Mrs. Varian came to him.

"I want you to go right down to New York," she told him, "and get me a hundred thousand dollars in cash. Now, don't raise objections, for I should only combat them, and it takes my strength so to argue with you. My husband's fortune is mine. There is no one to dictate to me how I shall use it. I want,—I insist upon this sum in cash, or some sort of bonds or securities that may be cashed by anybody, without identification. Oh, you know what I mean,—I want the money in such shape that these kidnappers will take it willingly. Of course, they won't accept checks or notes. Go on, now, Rodney, get off at once, and get back as soon as you can. And I want some man to stay in this house while you're away. I'm not exactly timid, but I've never stayed nights in a house without a man in it,— beside the butler, I mean,—and I'm sure you can invite some friend who would be willing to come. Perhaps Mr. Landon. He's so nice, and I'd try to make it pleasant for him in any way I could. There are plenty of books, and with good cigars, he might be contented."

"Oh, he'd be contented, all right; but Landon's gone off on a little trip. He won't be back for several days. How'd you like to have North? Probably he'd come."

"Very well,—if he's perfectly willing. I'd hate to bore him. You'll be back,—when?"

"I'll have to be away two nights,—if North can't come, there's young Clark,—he's a good sort."

"I hate to ask it of any of them, but I hate worse to stay alone. I'd get nervous and I shouldn't sleep at all."

"That's all right, Mrs. Varian, I know how you feel about it, and I'll get somebody."

Granniss was as good as his word, and, finding that Lawrence North was glad to do anything in his power to help Mrs. Varian, it was arranged that he should visit at Headland House until Rodney could get back from New York.

"But promise me," Granniss said, "that if you get further letters from the kidnappers you won't do anything definite until I return."

"I can't," said Minna, thoughtfully. "I wouldn't promise, anyway, but, as you must see for yourself, I can't do anything till I get that money."

"I suppose not," Granniss agreed, and went off. During a sociable and chatty evening, Minna told North about the letter from the abductors.

"Oh Mrs. Varian," he exclaimed, "you don't believe it, do you? I only wonder you haven't had several. It's a common way of crooks to attempt to get money."

"But this rings so true," Minna defended herself, and showed him the letter.

North studied it.

"It sounds plausible enough," he said, "but how is it possible? How could anyone have kidnapped the girl?"

"Now, look here, Mr. North, don't say over and over again, 'how could he?' You know somebody or something is responsible for Betty's disappearance as well as for Mr. Varian's death. Don't think for a minute that my anxiety about my daughter in any way obliterates or lessens my grief at my husband's death. But, as you must see, nothing can bring Mr. Varian back. While,—something may bring Betty back! Can you wonder, then, that I catch at any straw,—believe in any hope,—take up with any suggestion on the mere chance of getting my child back?

If they had asked for my whole fortune, I should pay it,— on the chance!"

"Yes," North spoke slowly,—"I see how you feel about it,—but you ought to have some proof that they really have your Betty."

"I've thought about that," Minna shuddered, "but, I've read of these cases, and—when they send a proof— sometimes, it's a—a finger—you know—"

"Oh, now, now, don't be morbid! I don't mean anything of that sort. But if they would give you a bit of her hair, or a scrap of her own handwriting—"

"But how can I demand that? How can I ask for it?"

"You just wait for their next instruction. If they are sincere in this offer, if they really have Miss Betty and are really ready to negotiate, they must tell you what to do next. And, Mrs. Varian, I advise you to do it. It may be a wrong principle, but your case is exceptional,—and, since you've showed me this letter, I can't help feeling it's the real thing. For one thing, you can see it's written by at least a fairly well educated man. I mean, not by the common, ignorant class. Moreover, the very audacity of demanding such enormous ransom, indicates to my mind that the writer can perform his part of the bargain. A mere crook, writing a fake letter, would never dream of asking such a sum. How are you going to manage the payment?"

"If you mean the method of handing it over, I don't know. I shall do as I'm directed. If you mean how shall I obtain the cash, I've asked Mr. Granniss to bring it up from New York for me."

"Is he going to travel home with that sum on his person!"

"Yes, he said he had no fear in that direction."

"Oh, no; since no one knows of it, he runs little risk."

Meantime, Rodney Granniss, in New York, was putting through his errands in record time.

He attended to the money matter, and by the aid of some influential friends of the Varian family, he obtained the desired sum in cash and unregistered bonds.

Then he went to see Pennington Wise.

That astute detective declared himself too busy to accept any new commission. But after Granniss had personally told the astonishing details of the case, Wise was unable to resist the temptation to undertake its investigation.

"The way you put it, Mr. Granniss," he said, "it sounds like an impossible condition. I can't see any explanation at all, but, as we know, there must be one. The obvious solution is a secret passage, but since you tell me there is none, I feel I must go up there and see for myself what could have happened."

"Then you'll come?"

"Yes,—I'll drop all else, and go straight off. We won't travel together, though. You go ahead, right now, and I'll follow soon. And, by the way,—you're carrying that money with you?"

"Yes."

"Let me take it. It's far safer so."

Rod Granniss opened his eyes wide. Was this strange man asking him to transfer his trusted errand to him?

Wise laughed. "I can't say I blame you for not wanting to hand it over. But, this I do tell you,—it will be safe with me,—and it may not be with you."

"Why, nobody knows I have it!"

"Even so. I strongly advise your letting me take it,— but you must do as you choose."

"You'll get it safely up to Mrs. Varian?" Granniss said, reluctantly producing the rather bulky parcel.

"Yes, I will,—and if I don't,—I'll make the loss good."

He looked meaningly at the younger man, and, flushing a little, Rodney said, "That's right,—Mr Wise. I couldn't make it good if I lost it. Take it."

And with no further security than the detective's word, Granniss handed over the money.

He went to his train in a most perturbed spirit. Had he done right or not? It all depended on the fidelity of the detective. To be sure, Granniss had every confidence in him, but the sum of money was so large that it might well prove a temptation to hitherto impeccable honesty.

He boarded his train, still uncertain of the wisdom of his course, and more uncertain as to what Mrs. Varian would say.

But, he reasoned, if they were to employ the services of one of the best and best known detectives in the country, it was surely right to obey his first bit of advice.

This thought comforted Granniss somewhat, and he was further comforted by an event which took place that night, and which proved the wisdom of (he detective's advice.

Granniss was asleep in his lower berth when the merest feeling of a cautious movement above awakened him.

He could hear no sound, but through half closed eyes, he saw the occupant of the berth above crawl silently down and stealthily reach for Rodney's clothes, which were folded at the foot of the berth.

Interested rather than afraid, Granniss watched the performance, keeping his own eyes nearly closed. It was too dark for him to see the marauder, who worked entirely by feeling, and who swiftly examined the clothing of his victim and then turned his attention to his bag.

Still Granniss made no sign, for he preferred to see the chagrin of the robber rather than to interrupt him at his work.

The bag yielded nothing of interest, and then the upper berth man came along and slipped his hand under Granniss' pillow.

Deftly done as it was, Rodney shot out his own hand and grabbed the wrist of the other. But it was twisted away from him, and in an instant the man was back in his own berth.

Rod thought it over, and concluded to raise no outcry. In the morning he would see who his visitor was, and then take such steps as he thought best. He fell asleep, and when he awoke the sun was up and his would be robber had disappeared. Chagrined at his own stupidity in over sleeping, but rejoiced at the safety of Mrs. Varian's money, Granniss went on with his journey home.

But, when he found on the floor of the car a handkerchief that had been under his pillow, he realized that a still further search for treasure had been made beneath his sleeping head.

CHAPTER 9: POOR MARTHA

WHEN Granniss stepped off the train at Headland Harbor, there were but few other passengers who alighted at the same time. But one of these, a mild young man, came nearer Rodney and said, quietly:

"Mr Granniss, may I speak to you a moment?"

"Certainly," Rod answered, after a quick glance at him.

"I am a messenger from Mr. Wise. I have with me the money for Mrs. Varian. Shall I give it to you here, or go up to the house with you and carry it? No one seems to be observing us; take it if you like."

Rodney stared at him. Wise, then, had sent his messenger with the money along on the same train. By this means he had outwitted the man in the upper berth, who, without question, knew of Granniss' errand, and who had thus been foiled in his attempt to rob him.

"Good for you!" Granniss exclaimed, heartily. "I think it will be all right for me to take it now,—here is the Varian car. "But would you prefer to go up to the house?"

"No; I'd rather not. I'm sure the way is clear now. I saw that performance in the train last night. But don't talk any more about it. Just take the box, and I'll go right back on the next train. Mr. Wise will arrive tomorrow."

Marveling at the detective's way of managing, Granniss took the unimportant looking parcel the young man offered, and with a brief good by, got into the Varian car.

The car could go only to the lodge gate, and from there Rodney trudged up the steep path to the house, half afraid that some bandit would even yet appear to rob him of the treasure.

But nothing untoward happened, and he reached Headland House in safety.

It was nearly noon when he arrived, and Lawrence North, still there, was as eager as Minna to hear the results of Granniss' errands in New York.

But not until after luncheon, when the three were alone in the library, did he tell the whole story.

He then gave a frank account of the detective's asking to take charge of the package of money, and of the lucky stroke it was that he did so.

"But I never imagined," Rodney said, "that he would send it along by a messenger on the same train!"

"Clever work!" said North. "Now, Mrs. Varian, have you a really good safe?"

"Yes, I have. My husband had it sent up here with our trunks. It looks like a wardrobe trunk, but it is a modern and secure safe."

The safe was in a closet in the library, and as the men examined it, they agreed that it was a good safe and proof against even a most skilful burglar.

"Unless he carries it off," suggested North. "It's not very large."

"But it's very heavy," Minna said, "and besides, it's clamped to the floor."

They put the parcel of money in the safe, tucked it well back behind less important matters, and Minna herself closed the door.

"I'll use the same combination Fred used," she said, "nobody on earth knows it but myself."

"Keep it to yourself, Mrs. Varian," North counseled her, "a secret shared is no secret."

"I'm not afraid to trust you two," Minna returned, "but I won't tell any one else.

"You've had no further communication from the kidnappers?" asked Granniss.

"I have," she said, "a letter came In this morning's mail. I don't know what to do about it. It's so strange,—

and yet,—I feel a positive conviction that I ought to do as they tell me."

"Whatever they ask, I beg of you not to decide until Mr. Wise gets here," Rodney said, earnestly.

"Since I have seen him, I know he will help us, and I feel sure that he would disapprove of your going ahead with this until he can advise you."

"What do they ask you to do?" North inquired; "that is, if you care to tell us."

"Oh, I'm glad to tell you, and see what you think. I know it might be a better plan to wait for Mr. Wise's arrival, but that may scare off these people and lose me my one and only chance to meet their demands,—and— get my Betty!"

"Where's the letter?" asked Granniss, looking very serious.

Minna handed him a paper, and the two men read it at the same time.

"This is your one and only chance to get back your daughter. Unless you obey these directions exactly and secretly you have no chance at all. At midnight, tonight, take the packet of money, if you have it, and drop it over the cliff into the sea. First you must place it in a light pasteboard box that is too large for it. This will insure its floating until we can pick it up. Now if you have told any one of this and if there is any boat on the sea at that time, we will not carry out our plans, the money will be lost and your daughter will be killed. So, take your choice of acting in good faith or losing your child forever. We are desperately in earnest and this is your one and only chance. If you fear to go to the cliff's edge alone, you may take a companion but only one who is in your faith and confidence. If you breathe a word to the police we shall know of it, and we will call off all our arrangements. It is up to you."

There was no signature. The paper and typing were like those of the previous letter from the same source, and the tenor of the letter seemed to be an ultimatum.

"Don't think of it for a minute," urged Granniss. "You are simply throwing away a large sum of money and you cannot possibly get any return. If the thing were genuine, if it were from real kidnappers who really had Betty, they would have given you a sign, a proof that they have her. They would have enclosed a scrap of her handwriting or some such thing. That telegram is of course a fake! This letter proves it!"

North looked dubious.

"You may be right, Granniss," he said, "perhaps you are. But,—I can't help thinking there may be some way to foil these people. Suppose Mrs. Varian throws a faked packet over the cliff—"

"No," Granniss declared, "that would do no good."

"Wait a minute," North went on; "then we could have a swift motor boat hidden in the shadows, and follow the boat that picks it up,—for I have no doubt that they will come for the money in a motor boat."

"Of course they'll do that," Rod agreed, "but it will be a boat more powerful than any we have around here—"

"Anyway," broke in Minna, "I won't play them false. I shall either follow their instructions in good faith, or not do it at all. I'm sure if I try to fool them, they'll take it out on Betty." She began to cry, and North said, hastily:

"Don't let me influence you, Mrs. Varian. You must do just as you please in the matter. If you feel that the mere chance of getting Betty by such means is sufficient to justify your equal chance of losing all that money,—you must follow your own wishes."

Minna Varian sat for several moments in deep thought. Then she said, quietly: "I've made up my mind. I shall not do this thing tonight. I am more influenced by Rodney's remark about the telegram than anything else. As he says, if these people really had Betty, they would send a note in her writing and not a telegram."

"That's the way to look at it, Mrs. Varian," cried Granniss, much pleased at her logical decision. "The telegram was a mistake on their part. To begin with, if Betty is closely confined, which she must be, if there's any truth at all in this matter, how could she get out to send a telegram? And if they sent it for her,—why not a note?"

"That's all true," said North, thoughtfully; "and when Mr. Wise gets here, he can doubtless discern the real truth of it all. The money will be all right in the safe over night, and tomorrow the detective can look after it. Then you're decided, Mrs. Varian?"

"I'm decided for the present, " she smiled a little; "but I don't say I won't change my mind. It's a terrible temptation to do as they bid me, even if it proves a false hope."

North went away, and poor Minna spent the rest of that day in alternate decisions for and against the directions of the kidnappers.

Granniss tried his best to dissuade her from what he deemed a foolish deed.

"To begin with," he argued, "I can't believe in kidnappers. How could they have abducted Betty, in broad daylight, with half a dozen people looking for her to come out of the house?"

"I don't know," said poor Minna, dejectedly, "but oh, Rodney, it doesn't mean anything to ask such questions as that! For how could any other thing happen? I mean, how do you explain Betty's disappearance without being kidnapped, any more easily than by such means? How explain Fred's death? How explain anything? Now, the only chance,—as the letter says,—is this plan of theirs. Shall I try it?"

"Look at it this way, Mrs. Varian," Granniss said at last. "Suppose you throw that money over the cliff. It's by no means certain that they will retrieve it safely."

"But that's their business. It's full moon now, and at twelve o'clock the sea will be bright as day. There'll be no spying boat around at that hour, and they will watch the box fall, get it quickly, and go away. Then they will send Betty back!"

Minna's face always lighted up with a happy radiance when she spoke of the return of Betty.

"But think a minute. Suppose by some chance they don't get the money,—suppose there is some stray boat out at that hour. Suppose the parcel gets caught on the way down—"

"It can't if I drop it right down from the overhang. And I'd have you to protect and watch over my own safety,—oh, Rodney, I *must* do it!"

And so, despite Granniss' dissuasion, in defiance of her own misgivings as to the genuineness of the anonymous bargainers, the poor distracted mother made up her mind to take the slim chance of recovering her lost child by the desperate method offered her.

But an unforeseen difficulty prevented her.

Shortly before midnight the sky clouded over and became entirely black. A terrific thunderstorm followed, and when that was over the whole heavens remained darkened and a drizzling rain kept up.

"It's out of the question," Granniss said, as the clock struck twelve. "It's still raining, it's pitch dark, nobody could see a parcel dropped over the cliffs, and you might lose your own life in the process. But, let this comfort you, if these people are really the kidnappers, they will give you another chance. They won't lose their chance of a fortune for a rainstorm, and they'll communicate with you again."

"That's probably true, Rod," and Minna gave a sigh of relief as she gazed out of the window at the rain. "And so, let's go to rest and try to hope for a future opportunity."

Mrs. Fletcher was waiting to put her patient to bed, and was much displeased at her late hour of retiring.

So, little was said by either of the women, and at last with a curt good night, the nurse went away to her own room, and Minna closed the door between.

But she could not sleep, she was restless and nervous.

At last she began to worry over the safety of the money in the safe. She imagined the thwarted kidnappers, disappointed at the collapse of their plans, coming up to the house to rob her of the money they had reason to suppose she had in her possession.

To her anxious and worried mind, it seemed the money would be safer up in her own room than down in the library safe.

On a sudden impulse she determined to go down stairs and get it. She donned dressing gown and slippers and stealthily, not to awake Fletcher, she crept down the stairs.

Into the library she went and, opening the closet door, began to work the combination that unlocked the safe.

Absorbed in her occupation, she did not hear a slight noise behind her. But suddenly a voice said, softly, "Oh, it's you, ma'am! I thought it was a robber!"

Minna turned quickly to see Martha, the waitress, staring at her.

As she already had the safe door open and was about to take out the parcel she was after, she was annoyed at any interruption.

"Martha!" she exclaimed, though in a low whisper, "what are you doing here? Go back to bed!"

"Yes, ma'am. I thought I heard robbers, ma'am."

"No; it's only I. I have to see about some important papers, and I can't sleep, so I'm attending to it now. Go back to your room at once, Martha."

"Yes, ma'am," and the girl obeyed.

Drawing a sigh of relief, Minna took her precious parcel, shut the safe, and went softly back to her own room. She put the package beneath her mattress, locked her bedroom door, and soon fell asleep, worn out with weariness and exhaustion.

"Great doin's," grumbled the cook, as Martha, who shared her room, returned to it, "where you been?"

"Hush up," said Martha. "I heard a noise and I thought it was burglars."

"And you went downstairs!" exclaimed Hannah. "Why, what foolishness! They might 'a' shot you!"

"There wasn't any," Martha explained. "It was Mrs. Varian, poking about in her safe."

"The pore leddy," said Hannah, sympathetically; "she can't sleep at all, at all. The nurse tells me she lies awake nearly all night and only gets forty winks in the morning after sun up."

"Well, she was a bit upset at my coming in," said Martha. "I wouldn't 'a' gone, only I thought it was my duty."

"Oh, you and your duty!" growled the cook. "I'm thinkin' your duty is to keep quiet and let me get a bit of sleep myself. I can't do without it as you and the missus can!"

Hannah grunted as she turned over and promptly went to sleep again, while Martha, who was both imaginative and curious of mind, lay awake, wondering what fearful things had happened or would happen to this strange house.

The girl was of a fearless nature, but deeply interested in the mysterious, and had more than once made investigations herself in an effort to find some secret passage such as the family were continually discussing.

But she had found nothing, and now, still unable to sleep, she occupied her mind in trying to form some new theory of the tragedies of Headland House.

Hannah awakened in the morning by reason of the alarm sounding from her bedroom clock.

"My goodness," she growled, to herself, "seems like I'd only just dropped to sleep. Well,—I've got to get up. Hey, Martha, come along, my girl."

But no response came from the other bed, and Hannah stepped across the room to give the girl an arousing shake.

"Why, heaven bless us, she ain't here!" exclaimed the startled cook. "Now, don't that beat all! Not content with rampoosin' round the house in the night, she must be up and off early in the mornin'! She thinks she's able to help them as has the detective work in charge! That Martha'"

Hannah proceeded to make her toilet and then descended the back stairs to the kitchen.

But on reaching the kitchen she gave voice to such a scream as could be heard by all the servants in the house, and even penetrated to the rooms occupied by Minna and her nurse.

"Whatever is the matter?" cried Fletcher, running out to the hall in her night clothes.

"Matter enough," Hannah called back. "Will you get Mr. Granniss, and tell him to come quick!"

Stunned by the cook's voice and manner, the nurse hurriedly knocked at Rodney's door, and he responded at once.

He was partly dressed, and finishing a hasty toilet, he ran down stairs.

He found Hannah, and Kelly, the butler, gazing at a huddled heap on the kitchen floor, which he saw at once, was the dead body of Martha, the waitress.

"What does it mean?" he asked, in an awed voice. "Who did it?"

"Who, indeed, sir?" Hannah said, whimpering like a child. "Oh, Mr. Granniss, sir, do get Mrs. Varian to go away from this accursed house! Nobody is safe here! I'm leaving as soon's I can pack up. Kelly, here, is going, too,—and I hope the missus will go this very day. It's curst indeed, is this place! Oh, Martha, me little girl,— who could 'a' done this to ye?"

Going nearer, Rodney looked at the body, touched it and felt for the girl's heart.

There was no heartbeat and the cold flesh proved her death took place some hours since.

"What do you know about it?" he asked the cook.

"Not a thing, sir. Martha was down stairs late last night, and she came up again, saying Mrs. Varian was down in the library."

"Mrs Varian down stairs! At what time was this?"

" 'Long about one o'clock, sir. Then me and Marthu both went to sleep,—leastways, I did, and that's all I knew till morning. Then I went to call the girl to get up, and her bed was empty. I came down—and here I saw—this!"

Throwing her apron over her face, Hannah rocked back and forth in her chair.

Rodney forced himself to think,—to give orders. "Hannah," he said, "I'm sorry, but we mustn't touch Martha,—and you'll have to get breakfast,—just the same."

"I can't, sir—I can't get the breakfast, with that poor dead girl,—why, I loved that young one like she was my own."

"But, Hannah, remember your duty to Mrs. Varian. Now, we'll lay a coverlet over Martha, and you and Kelly between you must prepare the coffee, and such things as Mrs. Varian wants. Be brave now, for there's enough sorrow for Mrs. Varian to bear. You and Kelly must do whatever you can to help."

Then Rodney looked hastily at all the doors and windows, finding them all securely fastened, as they always were at night.

"Thank goodness, Wise is coming today," he thought, as he went to telephone for Sheriff Potter again.

Potter summoned, he turned his mind to the question of how best to tell the news to Minna, and concluded to tell Nurse Fletcher first.

She came down then, greatly excited, to learn what had happened.

Granniss told her, and then said, "Now, Mrs. Fletcher, I beg of you, don't threaten to leave. Mrs. Varian needs you now more than ever, and as Mr. Wise, the great detective, is coming today, I'm sure you need not be afraid to stay on."

"Very well," Fletcher returned, primly, "I know my duty, and I propose to do it. I will stay with Mrs. Varian until she can get some one else,—or until I can get some one else for her,—but not an hour longer. How did the maid die?"

"I don't know, exactly," Rodney looked puzzled. "I didn't think it best to touch the body, except to convince myself that she is really dead. Now, will you tell Mrs. Varian, or shall I?"

"I'll tell her,—but I'd like you to stand by." So, taking Minna's breakfast tray, quite as usual, the nurse went back to her patient.

"You needn't tell me," was the greeting she received. "I overheard enough to know what has happened. It's awful,—but I suppose it's only the beginning of a further string of tragedies."

The utter hopelessness of the white face alarmed Granniss more than a hysterical outburst would have done.

"Now, Mrs. Varian," he said, consolingly, "it is an awful occurrence, but in comparison with your nearer sorrows, it means little to you. Try not to think about it; leave it to us and trust me to do all that is necessary or possible."

Potter arrived then, and Granniss went down to receive him.

"Another!" the sheriff exclaimed. "What devil's work is going on here, any way?"

He went to the kitchen and knelt beside the dead girl.

"Strangled," he said, briefly, after an examination. "Choked to death by a strong pair of man's hands. Mr. Granniss, I accuse you of the murder of this girl!"

CHAPTER 10: PENNINGTON WISE

GRANNISS looked at the constable blankly. Then he said, "Oh, well, you may as well accuse me as anybody, for the present. Where's Dunn?"

"He's coming," replied Potter, angry at the young man's indifference to his charge. "But you can't treat this matter so scornfully, Mr. Granniss. I've been thinking a whole lot about you in connection with all these mysteries up here, and I'm of the opinion you know more about some things than you admit."

"Quite right, I do," said Rod, cheerfully. "But don't arrest me just yet, for a really worth while detective is coming this morning and he may disagree with your conclusions. But this is a bad thing,—about this poor girl. I can't understand it."

"I can," and Potter looked straight at him. "You found her in your way and—you put her out of it."

"Oh, come now, Sheriff," this from Bill Dunn, who had come hurrying in, "don't go off half primed! You haven't any evidence against Mr. Granniss, except that he was in the house."

"I will have, though!" Potter muttered. "Where's the butler?"

"Here I am," and Kelly put in his appearance.

"Who saw this girl last?" Potter thundered, glaring round at the assembled members of the household. They were all present, for Nurse Fletcher had been unable to resist her aroused curiosity, and Minna Varian, too, stood in the background, composed and quiet, but evidently holding herself together by a strong effort of will power.

"I did," said Hannah, who stood, silent and grim, with folded arms, watching the sheriff.

"Where was she, then?"

"In her bed,—last night after midnight. She had been down stairs,—"

"After midnight?"

"Yes. She heard somebody down stairs, and—Martha was a brave one! She thought it was robbers in the house and she went down to see."

"Well?"

"Well, it was Mrs. Varian, who had gone down to the library. So Martha came up again,—"

"Leaving Mrs. Varian down there?"

"Yes," Minna interrupted, "leaving me down there."

"What were you doing, Mrs. Varian?"

"I was wakeful, and I went down to the library to look over some papers."

"And this girl came to you there? Tell the story in your own way."

"There's little to tell. I was startled at Martha's unexpected appearance, and sent her back to her room. Shortly afterward, I went back to my own room. That is all."

"Then Martha must have come down stairs again."

"That is quite evident," said Minna, looking sorrowfully at the dead girl. "Oh, Mr. Potter,—Rodney,— what does it all mean?"

"It will take a lot of clearing up, ma'am, before anybody can say what it means. Where were you at this time, Kelly?"

"In my own room, asleep," answered the butler.

"You heard nothing of the goings on?"

"No; my room is up in the third story, and I sleep very soundly."

"Humph! You do? Well, how about the doors and windows? I suppose they were locked and barred as usual?"

"Yes, they were," asserted Kelly. "I always look after those,—especially nowadays."

"Then there was no way for an intruder to get in this house, last night, between midnight, say, and morning?"

"No way, sir," assented Kelly.

"Then this girl was murdered by either you, Kelly, or by Mr. Granniss. Those marks on her throat of a strangling hold, were made by a man,—and by a strong man. Either of you two could have done it,—now, which one did?"

"Not I, sir," Kelly denied, as calmly as if he were merely refuting a slight accusation. "I know nothing about it."

"I don't believe you do," said Potter, judicially, "but I do think you're implicated, Mr. Granniss. Were you in your room all night?"

"Of course I was. I retired about one o'clock, and I didn't open my door again until I was summoned this morning to learn of Martha's death."

"You say that glibly enough,—but it will take some proof."

"No; your denial of it, or suspicion of my veracity will take the proof. Can you produce it?"

"You're not wise to be so cocksure, sir. There is such a thing as elimination, and I say that only you could have done this thing. The women are not capable of such a deed, and I've no reason to suspect Kelly."

"And just what is your reason for suspecting me?" Rodney's eyes were beginning to grow stern and his jaw set firmly. "Also, what evidence have you for your suspicions?"

"Come off, Potter," Bill Dunn warned him. "You ain't got no real evidence against Mr. Granniss, and you'd better go easy. To my mind, Mr. Granniss ain't going to kill a servant girl without a good reason."

"He may have a very good reason. Suppose Mr. Granniss was at the safe and suppose Martha surprised him there as she had startled Mrs. Varian. And suppose Mr. Granniss didn't want it known that he had been there, so he took the only sure method of silencing her lips."

"And what would Mr. Granniss be doing at the safe?" asked Dunn.

"Well, I happen to know that there was considerable of value in that safe last night."

Rodney started. How did the sheriff know that? But he said, "This is aside the mark, Mr. Potter. For Mrs. Varian has trusted me with the combination of the safe. I can open it at any time without let or hindrance. Why, then, should I sneak down in the middle of the night to do so?"

"For the very good reason that you wanted to take the money that was there and make off with it."

"And did I get it?"

"I should say not," declared Potter, "since you are still here!" He looked proud of this triumph of deduction, and went on:

"You had some valuables in that safe last night, Mrs. Varian, did you not?"

"Yes," replied Minna, almost smiling at the trend of the questions.

"Are they there now?"

"No, they are not—"

"Aha! What did I tell you?"

"But they are not there, because when I visited the library late last night, I took them away to my room for better protection of them."

"Oh!" Potter looked deeply chagrined. "You have them safe, then?"

"Oh, yes, quite safe, thank you."

"Well, all the same, went on the sheriff, doggedly, "Mr Granniss thought they were there, and went down to steal them."

"Maybe Martha was there on the same errand," said Dunn, thoughtfully.

"Don't you dare say a word against that pore dead child," cried Hannah, resenting at once any aspersion of her friend. "She would never dream of such a thing."

"What did she come down for, then?" asked Potter. "She had been down and had spoken to Mrs. Varian. Then she returned to her room, you say, and went back to bed. Now, why did she go down again?"

"That I do not know," Hannah said, belligerently, "but it was for no wrong purpose. Maybe she thought again she heard burglars, and maybe,—this time she was not mistaken."

"That would be a fine theory," Potter observed, "but for the fact that a burglar couldn't get in or out. So if she heard any one prowling about it must have been some member of the household. Isn't she a very daring young person?"

"She was afraid of nothing," Hannah stated. "She was great for detective stories, and she was crazy to investigate and inquire into all the goin's on of this terrible house! Martha was a dabster at puzzles. She was terrible quick witted, and sensed out everything—like a ferret! I never saw her beat at findin' out things!"

"That would explain why an evil doer, if there was one, would put her out of the way rather than have her live to tell of his depredations."

"All right, sir," Hannah conceded, "if so be's you put it that way. But don't you accuse that innocent girl of any wrongdoings herself, for she never did! Never."

"It does look that way," Rodney said, thoughtfully. "If Martha had that investigating proclivity, that would explain her reappearance down stairs,—that is, if there was a burglar,—yet, how could there be one? As usual, we're reasoning round in a circle. Now, Mr. Potter, I think your conclusions are logical and probable, except in so far as they drag me into this thing. I didn't leave my room last night at all. But I shall be at your disposal any time you want to question me further on the subject. Now, I want to go to the library and attend to my daily routine of business matters. Also, Mr. Wise will arrive before noon, and perhaps his skill may be helpful to your inquest."

Shortly before noon Pennington Wise did arrive.

He brought with him a strange, almost weird little girl creature, who ran up the steps and into the house before him.

Granniss had opened the door to them, and after greeting Wise, he turned to the girl.

"My assistant," Wise said, carelessly. "Name, Zizi. Give her over to the housekeeper, she'll take care of herself. Where's the library—or living room?"

Quite apparently tired from the steep walk up the cliff, Wise sank into a chair that Rodney placed for him. They stayed in the hall, which was large and square, and was often used as a sitting room. Zizi, however, dropping her bag in the hall, darted toward the dining room and thence to the kitchen.

"Oh," she cried, to Hannah, "are you the cook? Do give me some tea and toast or something,—I'm famished! My heavens! Who's that?"

Zizi bent over the dead girl, whose body still lay on the kitchen floor.

Martha was clad only in a kimono, over her nightdress, and wore bedroom slippers but no stockings.

"Hopped out of bed and ran down suddenly, didn't she?" commented the strange girl. "Didn't even stop to pin up her hair. Must have heard somebody that she was pretty sure was burglaring, or she wouldn't have run down again on the chance of its being Mrs. Varian the second time."

"How do you know all about it?" asked Hannah, aghast, at the remarkable person that had invaded her kitchen. "But you're right! Martha was too cute to be caught in a mistake twice,—she must have been sure it was not Mrs. Varian again!"

"Your chauffeur, who met us at the train, told us about this poor girl." Zizi's black eyes snapped as she delicately touched the awful bruises on Martha's throat. "Small doubt what did for her! Brute!"

Kneeling down, she ran her tiny fingers lightly over the body, and finally scrutinized the hands.

"Look, Hannah," she said, quietly, and held open the left hand.

It showed a dark green streak, of some sort, that spread entirely across the palm.

"Paint?" asked Hannah, not specially interested. "Our porch chairs have been painted lately,—but I don't see how she got out on the porch. Though o' course, she could 'a' done so. That Martha."

Just then Potter and Bill Dunn returned, and said they were ready to take the body of the girl down to the village, where her parents lived.

"And a good job to get it out of this house," said Dunn. "I tell you, Potter, poor Martha's death has nothin' to do with those other horrors up here; and Mrs. Varian has all she can stagger under without the extra sorrow and trouble of a servant girl."

"Wait!" commanded Zizi, for her ringing tone was nothing less than commanding, "wait, till Mr. Wise sees this girl."

She ran for the detective, who came at once.

The sheriff gazed with eager curiosity at the great city detective, and sniffed to see that he was a mere human being after all. He saw only a good looking, well set up man, with chestnut hair, brushed back from a broad forehead, and sharp blue eyes that were kindly of expression but keen of observation.

"But the astute Bill Dunn saw more than this. He recognized the air of efficiency, the subtle hint of power, the whole effect of generalship which fairly emanated from this quiet mannered man.

There was no bustle about Pennington Wise, no self assertion, but to those blessed with perceptions he gave an instant impression of sure reasoning and inerrant judgment.

He glanced quickly at Zizi, caught the almost imperceptible motion of her own little bird claw of a hand,

and then, without seeming to notice her at all, he spoke genially to the two men, and nodded sympathetically at the cook.

And they all liked him. If asked why, they could not have told, but his manner and attitude were so friendly, his mien so inoffensive and his cordial acceptance of each of them was so pleasant that he was instantly in their good graces.

Even the sheriff, who had been fully prepared to dislike and distrust this city wizard, capitulated gladly, and was ready to subscribe to all his theories, deductions and decisions.

"Too bad," Wise said, with real feeling, as he knelt by Martha's side. And few could have seen, unmoved, the bright young face of the strong healthy girl who had been so brutally done to death.

Gently, he lifted her chin and examined the black bruises on her throat.

"Finger prints?" suggested Potter, eager to show the city man his familiarity with modern methods.

"Hardly," Wise said. "I doubt much could be learned that way,—the bruise is so deep. Perhaps there may be prints of the ruffian's hands on her clothing. You might try it out, Mr. Potter."

Then, while the two men were speaking to each other about the matter, Wise unobtrusively looked at the inside of the girl's hands.

On the left palm he saw the long smear of dark green, and after quick but careful scrutiny, he bent lower and smelled of it. Then he closed the dead hand and rose to his feet

"You may take away the body, Sheriff," he said, "so far as I am concerned. She has people?"

"Yes, sir. Parents and sisters. Oh, it's a sorry thing for them."

"It is so," and then Wise let his perceiving eyes roam over the kitchen.

"Have you searched the floor well for anything that may have been dropped?" he asked.

"Oh, yes," the sheriff answered. "That's all been done, Mr. Wise. We're plain country folks here, but we know a thing or two."

"I'm sure of that," Wise assented. "Did you look under the dresser and beneath that corner cupboard?"

"Well, no; we didn't think it necessary to go so far as that."

"Probably not; most likely not. Yet, I wish, Hannah, you'd get a broom and just run it under there."

"I'll do it," volunteered Kelly, who had come to the kitchen.

He brought a broom, and brushing under the two dressers, brought out some dust, some threads and shreds and two yellow beads.

"Martha's?" asked Wise, quietly, picking up the beads.

"No!" exclaimed Hannah, staring at them. "Miss Betty's!"

"Miss Varian's!" Wise was himself surprised.

"Yes, sir; the very ones she wore the day—the day she—was lost."

"I'll take charge of them," he said, simply, and put them in his pocket.

Kelly and his broom failed to find anything further, and suddenly realizing the side light it gave on her housekeeping habits, Hannah began to explain how everything was going at sixes and sevens of late.

"Of course it would," Zizi soothed her, as Wise returned to the hall. "Now, Hannah, tell me, did you find anywhere, any more of Miss Betty's beads?"

"I found two, when I was sweepin' here one day. But I slipped 'em in this drawer an' never remembered them again. Here they be."

She retrieved the two beads, and Zizi took them.

"Did she wear a long string of them?"

"No, miss, a fairly short string. About like that you've on yourself."

Zizi's modest little string of black beads hung perhaps four inches below her throat. She examined the yellow beads, saw they were of amber, and put them away in her little handbag.

"Now, Hannah," she went on, "you and I are friends "

"An' that I'm proud to be, miss!"

"And you must help me all you can—"

"Help you what?"

"Find out the truth about Miss Betty,—and perhaps,—find her."

"Are you,—are you—"

"Yes, I'm a detective,—that is, I'm the assistant of Mr. Wise, and he's the greatest detective in the world."

"Is he that, now?" and Kelly, unable to resist the fascination of this queer visitor, joined the group.

"Yes, he is. And he is going to solve the whole mystery,—if we all help. And, maybe we'll help best by doing nothing. And especially by saying nothing. So, you two keep quite still about finding these beads, won't you, and about matters in general. You talk over things with the villagers, I suppose, but don't say anything about what happens up here now. Discuss the past, all you like, but not the present. See?"

They didn't see clearly, but they were more than ready to promise whatever this girl asked, and then between the two, Zizi was served with such a luncheon as might have befitted a royal guest.

"Goodness, gracious, sakes alive!" she exclaimed, "don't bring me anything more, I beg of you. I shall go to sleep like an anaconda and not wake up for six months!"

Then, while the detective ate his luncheon at the table with Minna Varian and her secretary, Zizi went in search of the nurse.

She found Mrs. Fletcher eating her meal from a tray in her sitting room. It hurt her pride to do this, but Minna Varian declared that she saw quite enough of Fletcher between meals and must have some respite.

"Nice to eat alone, I think," was Zizi's observation as she entered, uninvited, and perched herself on the arm of a nearby chair.

"You're Fletcher, aren't you? Now, won't you please tell me some things confidentially? I see, you're a woman of deep perceptions, and are not to be caught napping. Tell me, do you think Mrs. Varian went down stairs a second time last night?"

"That she did not," asserted the nurse. She was flattered at Zizi's attitude and would have told her anything she asked.

"How do you know?"

"I can't go to sleep myself, you see, till Mrs. Varian is asleep. So I always wait until I hear her steady breathing before I let myself drop off."

The statement was too surely true to be disbelieved and Zizi went on.

"Then who was it that Martha heard downstairs, that she went down a second time?"

"Maybe she didn't hear anybody. Maybe she went down to see what she could pick up herself—"

"Steal, do you mean? Oh, for shame! To accuse a poor, dead girl!"

Mrs Fletcher looked ashamed.

"I oughtn't to,—I s'pose. But, Miss, what else is there to think? I well know how this house is locked up of nights; nobody from outside could get in. The other servants are as honest as the day, and though I've no real reason to suspect Martha, yet there doesn't seem to be any other way to look,—does there, now?"

"Some way may turn up," said Zizi. "Tell me more about Betty,—Miss Varian."

"I can't tell you from having known her, for I never saw the girl, but since I've been taking care of Mrs. Varian there's little I don't know about the whole family. She's nervous, you know, and so she talks incessantly, when we're alone."

"Nothing, though, to cast any light on Miss Varian's disappearance?"

"Oh, no; nothing but sort of reminiscences about her husband and how good he was to her, and how she grieves for him,—and for her child. Poor woman,—it's fearful to hear her."

"It must be," said Zizi, sympathetically; "my heart bleeds for that poor tortured soul."

CHAPTER 11: CLUES

IT was after luncheon, in the library, that Pennington Wise began his real business of the investigation of the Varian mysteries.

First of all, he desired to look over the papers in Mr. Varian's desk, and with the assistance of Granniss, he was soon in possession of the principal facts to be learned that way.

Moreover, he discovered some things not yet taken into consideration by the local detectives, and he read with interest a number of letters that were carefully filed, apparently for preservation.

Rapidly he scanned them and tossed them aside, retaining a few for further consideration.

"I think, Mrs. Varian," he said, at last, that a most important fact in the case is the strange bequest of the Varian pearls to your husband's niece instead of to his daughter. Can you explain this?"

"I cannot," said Minna, "it seems to me absolutely unexplainable. For generations those pearls have descended from parent to child,—sometimes a mother owned them, sometimes a father, but they were always given to the oldest daughter, or, if there were no daughter, then to a son. Only in case of a childless inheritor did they go to a niece or nephew. Why my husband should so definitely bequeath them to his niece,—I cannot imagine. I've thought over that for hours, but I can't understand it. I will say frankly, that Betty and her father frequently had differences of opinion, but nothing more than many families have. They were really devoted to one another, but both were of decided, even obstinate nature, and when they disagreed they were apt to argue the matter out, and as a result of it, they did sometimes lose their temper and really quarreled. But it always blew over quickly and they were good friends again. I never paid any attention to their little squabbles, for I knew them both too well to think they were really at enmity. But this matter of the pearls looks as if my husband had a positive dislike for the child, and as a mark of spite or punishment left the pearls away from her. It makes little difference, if—if—"

"Don't think about that, Mrs. Varian," said Wise, kindly; "I'm considering this strange clause of Mr. Varian's will from the viewpoint of the whole mystery. It may prove a clue, you see. I want to say, right now, that the whole affair is the greatest and most baffling puzzle I have ever known of. The disappearance of your daughter and the death of your husband offer no solution that seems to me possible,—let alone probable. I can set up no theory that does not include a secret passage of some sort. And though I am emphatically informed there is none, yet, as you may imagine, I must investigate that for myself."

"I've found the house plans," said a low, thin little voice, and the strange girl, Zizi, appeared in the room. That slender little wisp of humanity had an uncanny way of being present and absent, suddenly, and without explanation. She was there, and then she wasn't there,— but her goings and comings were so noiseless and unobtrusive that they were never noticed.

Pennington Wise held out his hand without a word. Zizi gave over a bulky roll of papers and subsided.

Unrolling the time yellowed sheets, they saw that they really were the old contractor's plans of the house.

With a sigh of satisfaction Wise commenced to study them,—Granniss looking over his shoulder. Minna sat quietly, her nervousness lost in her eager anticipation of the new detective's successful quest.

The two men studied the plans carefully. "I wish North could see these," Rodney said; "he's of an architectural bent, Mr. Wise, and he measured the house all over, trying to find an unexplained bit of space. According to these plans, North is right, and there isn't any."

"I'm of an architectural bent myself," Wise smiled, "and I agree, there's no foot of room left unaccounted for on these papers. Of course a secret passage could have been built in, in contradiction of the plans, but I can't think there is any such, after your own search. It might be out of doors?"

"But we would have seen anyone going in or out of the house," Minna explained. "We were all watching."

"The back doors?"

"There's only one," Rodney told him. "And that was locked on the inside. Locked and bolted. No, whatever happened, nobody came in through the kitchen."

"Do you assume an intruder, then, Mr. Wise?" Minna asked.

"I am obliged to, Mrs. Varian. To begin with the only fact we can positively affirm, Mr. Varian was shot,—and not by his own hand. This we assume because of the absence of the weapon. Now, either Miss Betty shot him or someone else did. I can't think the daughter did it, for it's against the probabilities in every way,—though, of course, it's a possibility. But the difficulties in the way of explaining what the girl did with herself afterward, seem to me greater than the objections to assuming an intruder from outside. I mean from outside the family,—not from outside the house. The explanation of his entrance and exit is no more of a puzzle than the explanation of Miss Varian's exit. And I think we must dismiss the idea that the girl concealed herself in this house,—whether alive or—a suicide."

"The girl didn't do it," came Zizi's low murmur. She was sitting on an ottoman, near Minna, and now and then she caressed the hand of her hostess. "There's a big mind at the back of all this. And you're overlooking the death of the maid last night. Why, Penny, it's all of a piece."

"Yes"; and Wise roused himself from a brown study. "It is all of a piece, and it hinges on that bequest of the Varian pearls."

"Hinges on that?" said Zizi.

"I mean that's a key to the situation. When we learn why Mr. Varian made that strange arrangement, we'll be on our way to a solution of the mystery. But the first thing is to find Miss Varian."

"Oh, Mr. Wise," Minna cried out, "you think she is alive—"

"I very much hope so, and though I don't want to give you false encouragement, I can't help feeling that she may be."

"Yes, she is," came Zizi's quiet assurance, and Minna impulsively kissed her.

"What a comfort you are!" she exclaimed; "elf, pixie,— I don't know what to call you,—but you bring me courage and hope."

Zizi's great dark eyes gave appreciation, but she only said, "You're up against it, Penny."

"I am, indeed," Wise said, very gravely; "and my first work must be a deep investigation of all Mr. Varian's affairs. You were entirely in his confidence, Mrs. Varian?"

"Oh, yes; we had no secrets from one another. He told me all his financial ventures or business worries. There were none of those of late, but years ago, there were some. Yes, I may say I know everything that ever happened to my husband,"

"Then who has been blackmailing him of late, and what for?"

"Blackmail!" Minna looked blank. "Never such a thing as that has happened to my husband!" She spoke proudly and positively.

"You know of no one who had a hold over Mr. Varian,—or thought he had,—and who wrote him threatening letters?"

"Most assuredly not! And I know that nothing of the sort ever did occur, for he would most certainly have told me. We were more confidential than most married people, and we never had secrets from one another."

"Well, perhaps I am over imaginative."

"What made you think it?" asked Minna, curiously; "if you have found any letters you can't explain, show them to me,—I can doubtless tell you about them."

After a moment's hesitation, Wise handed her a letter. It bore neither date nor address, but it read,

"Unless you accede to my demands, I shall expose you, and the woman you robbed will claim redress or return of her property."

This brief message was signed "Step." and Minna read it with a look of utter perplexity.

"I don't know what it means," she said, handing it back, "but I'm sure it's of no importance. Mr. Varian never robbed a woman in his life! .The very idea is too absurd to consider. You are at liberty to hunt it down, Mr. Wise, but you will never find it has a meaning that will reflect on my husband's stainless honor! You may refer to any of his friends, his relatives or his business associates. All will tell you that Frederick Varian and dishonesty are contradictory terms!"

"That may all be true, Mrs. Varian, and doubtless is true, but you know blackmailers are not so scrupulous, and they sometimes find a peg to hang their demands on even in the case of the most upright. This note is undated, but the envelope shows it was mailed less than six months ago. Therefore the matter may be still unsettled, and may have a bearing on the whole case. Could there have been any family reason that would influence him to leave the pearls away from his daughter?"

"Oh, no! His brother and sister in law were quite as much surprised as I was to learn of that. But, Mr. Wise, what do you think about this matter of the kidnappers asking for ransom? Do you think it is all a fraud?"

"I'm going to look into that as soon as I can. At first glance, it seems fraudulent, but the wonder is that you haven't had similar letters from other fakers. However, I am going to work backward. I want, first of all to look about a bit, for evidences or clues regarding last night's tragedy. I am sure the whole string of horrors is a connected one, and to find out who killed poor Martha, will in my opinion be a stepping stone to the solution of the other mysteries.

"There's a clue for you, then," Zizi said, not moving from her seat, but pointing to a spot on the rug near the safe.

Wise's eyes followed her finger's direction and saw a slight mark, as of a dusty footprint.

In a moment, he was on his knees near it, and scrutinized it carefully.

"I've heard of footprint clues," said Granniss, interested, "but that is so vague and imperfect, I don't think you can deduce who made it,—can you?"

"Not from the print, " Wise said,—thoughtfully, and then added nothing to his unsatisfactory statement.

He then took a paper cutter from the desk, and scraped onto a bit of smooth paper what dust he could get from the footprint, and carefully folded it up and put it in his pocketbook.

"What shoes were you wearing when you visited the safe last night, Mrs. Varian?" he asked.

"Bedroom slippers," she replied.

"Had you walked anywhere except to traverse the halls and stairs, from your bedroom down here?"

"No, nowhere else."

"And you took that package of money up to your room with you?"

"Yes."

"Had you not done so, it would have been stolen," Wise said, calmly. "A thief visited this safe after you were here,—he thought the money was here. He was surprised by the maid, Martha, coming down to spy on him,—and in order to get rid of her,—and save himself, he strangled her."

All present stared at him, and Rodney Granniss flushed a deep red.

"To a disinterested observer, Mr. Wise," he said, "it might easily appear that I was that thief. I knew the money had been put in the safe. I did not know Mrs. Varian had removed it, I—"

"Look here," interrupted Zizi, "you talk too much! If you're going to be suspected, for the love of cheese, let somebody else do it! Don't meet trouble half way, and sing out, 'Pleased to meetcha!' Be careful, Mr. Granniss."

"Hush up, Zizi," Wise counseled her. "Children should be seen and not heard."

"All right, Penny, I'll be good. Now, here's a present for you."

She gave him the yellow beads given her by the cook.

"Divulge," he said, briefly, as he stared at the tiny objects in his palm.

But Minna Varian had caught sight of them and had recognized them. "Oh!" she cried, "Betty! *Betty!* Those are the beads she had on that day! Where did you get them? Where did they come from?"

And then, before they could answer her, her overwrought nerves gave way, her calm broke through the constraint she had put upon it, and she became hysterical.

Granniss went at once for Mrs. Fletcher, and the nurse took her patiently away.

"She'll be all right with Fletcher," Rodney said, returning after he had assisted Minna to her room; "it won't be a very bad attack, nurse thinks. Really, I've been surprised that Mrs. Varian has kept up as well as she has. Now, Mr. Wise, tell me what you suspect regarding Mr. Varian? And also, tell me if you suspect me—in any way. I plead not guilty,— and I want to add that Miss Varian and I are sweethearts. We couldn't call it an engagement for her father wouldn't hear of such a thing.

But we hoped to persuade him ia time,—and truly, I thought he would finally consent. I'm tailing you this, so you can see what a deep interest I havs in the recovery of Betty,—for I am not willing to believe she is dead. In fact, I believe she has been kidnapped, and though I'm not sure those letters Mrs. Varian has received are in good faith,—yet I believe she is being held for ransom."

"By whom?" asked Wise.

"By the kidnapper—"

"Who also is the—"

"Blackmailer!" said Zizi, in an awestruck voice. "Oh, Penny Wise, how you do jump at a solution! You just clear all intervening obstacles, and land on the truth!"

"I'm far from having landed," said Wise, ruefully; "that's all theory,—with very little fact to back it up."

"Well, these beads are facts," Zizi said. "They're two more. Penny, from the same string that you already have a few from. You see, Mr. Granniss," she said, turning to Rod, "Mr Wise discovered a few of these beads in the kitchen this morning, and a little later, I found that the cook had picked up two in the kitchen the day after Miss Betty's disappearance. The string of them that she wore was not a long one, but still there were at least a dozen or so more than we have found. Where are they?"

She had turned again to Wise as she put this question.

"I know the beads well," Granniss said, "but how did they get in the kitchen?"

"It may be a simple matter," Wise responded. "Perhaps the string broke when she was out there getting the lemonade. I understand all the servants were away."

"But, Penny," Zizi reminded him, "in that case the other beads would be about, somewhere. She would have picked them up and put them in a box or something."

"Yes, she would," Rodney agreed, "for Betty loved that necklace. She loved anything yellow. You've heard about the yellow pillow?"

"No," said Wise. "Do try, Mr. Granniss, to tell me everything. I was called to this case altogether too late. Much could have been done had I been here sooner. But, now tell me every little thing you can think of."

So Granniss told them of the finding of the yellow satin sofa pillow in the middle of the kitchen floor. He obtained the pillow from the hall and showed it to them.

Zizi scrutinized it with her eager black eyes, and carefully extracted from its embroidered design a small fine hairpin.

"An invisible," she said, holding it up to the light. "Betty's,—I daresay?"

"Yes," and Granniss looked at it. "She wore dinky little ones like that in her front hair. All girls do, I guess."

"It may mean something or nothing," Wise said, musingly. "If Miss Varian was in the habit of lying on the hall sofa, the hairpin may have been caught in the cushion some time ago."

"I don't know," Granniss said; "I never was here while—when Betty was here."

"Well, aside from the hairpin, what about the yellow pillow, on the kitchen floor, Penny?" Zizi asked, looking up into the detective's face as at an oracle.

"It's a clue, all right," Wise said; "oh, if I'd only been here that very day! A most astounding case, and every possible evidence wiped out!"

"Oh, no, not that," Zizi spoke cheerfully. "And now, as you say, you must get busy in the matter of poor Martha. What about the green streak?"

"Yes," the detective spoke to Rodney. "There was a dull green smear across the palm of that girl's left hand. I see no freshly painted furniture in this room."

"No, there wouldn't be," Zizi ruminated. "And it wasn't paint,—you know it wasn't."

"It looked like paint, and what else would remain there so indelibly?"

"What could it be anyway?" queried Granniss. "What do you suggest?"

"I can't think, myself," and Wise looked non plussed. "I smelled it, but there was no odor of paint. Nobody around the house uses watercolors, I suppose?"

"No," said Granniss.

"It was such a smear as might have been made by a paint brush filled with a dull green watercolor pigment,— but I don't say it was that."

"It was more like a vegetable stain," Zizi suggested. "A mark like that could have been made by grasping a dish or saucepan that had held spinach."

"Oh, come now, Zizi, that's a little farfetched."

"Not if we find cold spinach in the refrigerator," Zizi persisted. "Martha might have been getting something to eat."

"In that case the green smear doesn't count for much," Wise said. "But we have accumulated some clues. We have the yellow beads, the yellow pillow, the green streak, and last, but by no means least, the dust I scraped from the floor in this room."

"Explain the significance of that, won't you?" asked Granniss. "Or are you one of those secretive detectives?"

"Not at all That dust is, to my mind, from the shoe of the man who tried to rob this safe last night, thinking that money was in it. Now, I admit, Mr. Granniss, that you knew, or thought you did, that the money was there; you knew the combination; you are quite strong enough to have strangled a woman who surprised you at your job; yet I know you didn't have anything to do with the attempted robbery, because—"

"Because you love Betty!" Zizi said, softly, her eyes shining with sympathy and understanding.

"Right you are, Wise, go on—"

"Also, because," Wise went on, "because, I'm sure that is the footprint of the would be burglar, and while the footprint as a print is too indistinct to be a clue to the man who made it, yet the dust that forms the print is indicative. It is a fine dust made up of particles of cement. I mean such dust as would adhere to a shoe that had traversed a cement floor, and, more likely an imperfect cement floor."

"That means the cellar!" Rodney cried; "I've been down there a lot of late, poking around for that everlasting secret passage, and there's a lot of loose cement."

Wise gave him a quick glance, but his enthusiasm was so genuine, that the detective dismissed a sudden qualm of suspicion.

"Slip down and get me a sample, will you?" he said, and Granniss went at once.

"Big case, Zizi," Wise said, as the two were left alone.

But he spoke heavily, almost despairingly, and with no show of his usual exultant interest in a big case.

"Yes, but," the black eyes turned hopefully to his own, "there are tangible clues. And those of Betty's can wait. Do you chase those that have to do with Martha first."

"I certainly shall. Martha was killed by the burglar. Did he kidnap Betty?"

"And kill Mr. Varian?" Zizi added, and then Granniss returned.

He brought a little cellar floor dust in a paper, and, as Wise had expected, that and the particles he had scraped from the library rug, were indubitably the same.

"Well, then," Wise remarked, "the burglar came up from the cellar."

"Where he had been hiding, goodness knows how long!" Rodney exclaimed. "For we locked the house securely before we went upstairs."

"I think it's time I took a look at the cellar," said Wise, and all three started down.

Chapter 12: A Letter from Nowhere

PENNINGTON WISE himself assisted in the locking up of the house that night, for he was determined if any more burglars came, he would know how they got in. The money that Minna had in her possession he took charge of, saying he would be responsible for its safety.

Long the detective lay awake in his pleasant bedroom that overlooked the sea. He could hear the great waves tossing and breaking at the foot of the cliff and he couldn't free his mind from a queer obsession to the effect that those waves held the secret of the mysteries of Headland House.

"It's too absurd," he thought to himself in the darkness, "but I do feel that the whole matter is dependent in some way or other on the cliff and the sea."

Had he been asked to elucidate this more definitely he could not have done so. It was only a hunch,—but Wise's hunches were often worthy of consideration, and he determined to go out on the sea in somebody's boat when the morning came, and see if he could find any inspiration.

When the morning came it brought a fresh surprise.

The household assembled promptly for an eight o'clock breakfast. Minna Varian, pale and fragile looking, clad in a simple black house dress, was a strong contrast to the young and glowing vitality of Zizi, whose slim little black frock was touched here and there with henna, and whose vivid and expressive face needed no aid of cosmetics to be a bright, colorful picture in itself.

Wise was very grave and silent,—he was in a mood which Zizi knew was that of utter bafflement It was not often the detective felt this conviction of helplessness, but it had occurred before, and Zizi noted it with some alarm.

It meant desperate and wearing effort on Wise's part, deep thinking and dogged persistence in forming and proving theories, that more likely than not would prove false. It meant a strain of brain and nerves that might result in a physical breakdown,—for the detective had been working hard of late, and this impenetrable mystery seemed the last straw.

Granniss was the most serene of the quartette. He was young and hopeful. He was innocent of any crime or knowledge of it, and he cared naught for the half voiced suspicions of the local police. In fact, they had practically given up the case as far beyond their ken, and now that Wise was in charge, the sheriff wanted nothing to say in the matter, except when Wise desired to consult him.

And Granniss was confident that Wise would find Betty. He had no real reason for his belief in the detective's magic, but he had unbounded faith, and he was a born optimist. He felt sure that, if Betty had been killed, the fact would have become known by this time,— and if she were still alive, surely she would be found. He had come to believe in the kidnappers, and though he couldn't understand how the deed had been done, he cared more to get Betty back than to learn what had happened to her. Also, he was kept busy in attending to the daily influx of business letters and financial matters connected with the Varian estate. Doctor Varian had promised to come up to Headland House again as soon as he could, but he was a busy man and hadn't yet made time for the visit.

As breakfast was about to be served, Kelly brought a letter to Minna saying simply, "This was on the hall table when I came downstairs this morning, madam."

A glance showed Minna that it was from the same source as the other "ransom" letter, and she handed it unopened to Wise.

Staring hard at the envelope, he slit it open, and read the contents aloud.

"We know all that is going on. We have your daughter. You have the required sum of money. If you will bring about an exchange, we will do our part. Your fancy detective must work with you, or at least refrain from working against you, or there can be no deal. You may drop the package over the cliff, exactly as directed before, at midnight on Friday. Unless you accomplish this, in strict accordance with our orders, you will lose both the money and your child. One divergence from our directions and your daughter will be done away with. You can see we have no other way out. This is our last letter, and our final offer. Take it or leave it. Enclosed is a note from your daughter to prove that we are telling you the truth."

And enclosed was a small slip of paper on which was written,

"Mother, do as they tell you. Betty."

"Is that your daughter's writing?" Wise asked, as he passed the little note to Minna.

"Yes," she whispered, trembling so violently and turning so white, that Zizi flew to her side, and induced her to take a sip of coffee.

"Brace up, now, dear," Zizi said, "you'll need all your strength and all your pluck. And cheer up, too. If that's from Betty, she's alive, and if she's alive, we'll get her! Bank on that!"

Zizi's strong young voice and encouraging smile did as much as the coffee to invigorate and cheer the distracted mother, and Rod Granniss, said, "Sure! that's Betty's own writing,—no forgery about that! Now, Mr. Wise, what next?"

"Next, is to find out how that note got into this house," said Pennington Wise. "I locked up myself last night,—I listened but I heard no intruder's footstep, and I know no outside door or window was opened. It was,—it must have been an inside job. Kelly!"

"Yes, sir."

"Where were you all night?"

"In my bed, sir. On the third floor of the house."

"Oh, pouf! I know it wasn't you, Kelly, you could no more have engineered this letter than you could fly to the moon! And Hannah, I suppose was in her bed, too. I've no wish to question the servants,—they had nothing to do with it."

"It was the kidnappers, then?" Zizi asked, softly. "It was the kidnappers," Wise said. "They,—or he,—came into this house by some secret way, which we have got to find. They, or their agent, came in night before last to steal that money from the safe. Foiled in that attempt, they have returned to their ransom scheme, hoping to get the money that way. They are desperate, and,—I don't know, Mrs. Varian but that we'd better—"

"Oh, Penny," Zizi cried, "don't throw away all that money—"

"What is that sum,—any sum,—in comparison with getting my child?" cried Minna, so excited as to be with difficulty warding off a hysterical attack.

"But you wouldn't get her," Zizi asserted, positively. "First, they'd never get the money,—thrown down in the darkness like that,—it's too uncertain. And, if they did, they wouldn't return Betty,—I know they wouldn't."

"Never mind that now, Zizi," Wise spoke from deep preoccupation. "We have till Friday night to decide about it. Today is only Wednesday. What I hope to get at from this note is the identity of the kidnapper. I am sure it is the same man as the one who wrote that blackmail letter."

"This is typewritten," Granniss said, studying the letter. "And not signed in any way. I've heard, though, that typewriting is as easily distinguished or recognized as pen writing."

"That's true in a sense," Wise told him. "I mean, if you suspect a certain person or machine, you can check up the peculiarities of the script, and prove the typing. But in this case, the letter was doubtless written on some public machine,—say in a hotel or business office, and even if found, would give no clue to the writer. We have to do with the cleverest mind I have ever been up against. That is positive. Now the reason I connect the kidnapper and the blackmailer is twofold. First, if this man's blackmailing scheme proved unsuccessful, he may have struck at his victim in this more desperate way. And, second, there is a resemblance in the diction of the notes from the kidnappers and the note of blackmail intent, signed 'Step'."

"What do you suppose 'Step' means?" Granniss asked.

"Short for Stephen, I daresay," replied Wise. "There's no other name that begins,—oh, yes, there is Stepney,—but it doesn't matter. 'Step' is our man,—of that I'm sure. But how to find such an elusive individual is a puzzling problem."

"Then you believe there's a secret passage?" Granniss said.

"There simply has to be. It may be a hidden one it may be a false doorway or window frame, but there is most certainly a way for that villain to get in and out of this house at will. Now that way must be found, and at once or I give up my profession and make no further claim to detective ability!"

"We'll find it, Penny," Zizi promised him.

"Find it, if you have to tear down the whole house," Minna exclaimed, excitedly. She was nervously caressing the note from Betty, and was ready to further any project that was suggested.

"You don't own the house?" Wise asked.

"No; but I'll buy it. It's in the market, and the price is not so very high. Then you can tear it down, if you wish, and I can sell the ground afterward."

"Good business deal!" Granniss said. "I'd like nothing better than to drive a pick into these old walls."

"But there's no place to drive, with any expectation of success," Wise demurred. "Where's your friend North? Isn't he an architect? Can you get him up here?"

"Surely," Rod said, "I'll telephone him, if you say so. I'm sure he'll be glad to come. He isn't a professional architect, but he knows more about building plans than many a firm of contractors does."

"Call him, then, please, when you've finished your breakfast," Wise directed, and returned to his study of the letter.

"I can't understand it at all," he groaned to Zizi, after breakfast was over.

Minna had gone to her room, and Rodney was reading the mail.

Wise and Zizi were in the hall, sitting on the sofa with the yellow pillows.

"This figures in it," Zizi said, patting the yellow pillow that had held the little hairpin.

"As how?"

"Find that secret entrance first," she said, drawing her pretty brows together. "That will explain 'most everything. And, Penny, it isn't a secret passage, as they call it. It's just a concealed entrance."

"And through the cellar,—for you know, there was cellar dust on the library floor,—near the safe."

"That only proved the man had been down cellar, — hiding probably until the time was ripe. I've scoured that cellar myself."

"So have I, Zizi, and there's not a loose stone in its walls or a trap in its floor,—of that I'm certain."

"I'm sure of that, too; and Penny, I even went down the well."

"You did! You little rascal. They told me Dunn went down and examined that."

"Well, I had to go, too. It wasn't difficult,—the stone sides are easy to climb up and down. Not very slippery, either. But dirty! My, I ruined one of my pet dresses. Yet there was no hole in the old well sides. No missing stone or anything suspicious. And that settles the cellar!"

"I don't think the entrance is through the cellar. I incline more to the idea of a false door frame,—you know, the frame and all on hinges. Then, locking would not affect the opening of the whole affair."

"That's all right,—but, which door?"

"There are only two. I've examined them both. It may be a window."

"Get friend North to confab with you. You're clever enough, Penny, but you're not a real architect. Mr. North may have some suggestions to make, that with your ingenuity may work it out."

Lawrence North arrived and with him came Claire Blackwood. The latter was urged to the visit largely by curiosity to learn how things were going, and also by a desire to renew her expressions of sympathy and hope to Mrs. Varian.

Zizi managed to get a few words alone with Claire.

"Tell me about this Eleanor," the girl said. "I feel sure a lot hinges on that peculiar matter of the pearls. Is Eleanor a scheming sort?"

"Oh, no!" exclaimed Mrs. Blackwood. "She is a dear girl,—very young, and of a simple, charming nature. She was devoted to her cousin, and had no thought of the family pearls ever being hers. Don't for a moment think of Eleanor Varian as capable of the slightest thought of disloyalty, much less of envy or covetousness."

"Well, I just wanted to know," said Zizi, with her winning, confidential smile. "What about her parents? Could her mother have influenced Mr. Frederick Varian's mind against his own daughter?"

"No, indeed! Nor Doctor Varian either! Why, they're the best and finest kind of people, all of them. Whatever the explanation of those pearls being left away from Betty, it was not due to any maneuvering on the part of Eleanor or her parents! Of that you may be sure!"

Meantime, Lawrence North and the detective were discussing architecture. They were in the library and the plans of the house were spread out before them.

"I'm interested," North said, looking eagerly at the plans, "for I'm always fond of plans. And, too, I want to prove my contention that there's no space unaccounted for. At first, I thought there might be a bit of spare room between this wall and this,—you see. But that jamb is merely the back of a small cupboard in the hall. Can you find any hint of false building?"

"No; I can't," Wise admitted, and then he unfolded his theory of a double door frame,—or, rather a hinged door frame or window frame.

"That," said North, "must be looked for in the house, not on the plans. But I doubt it. Any such thing would be apt to show the joints after years of disuse. You see, this house hasn't been lived in before for a long time."

"Then I'll have to give up the notion of a double door," and Wise sighed. "Now, here's another matter. I want to go out in a boat,—a good motor boat, and have a look round the sea and the cliff and observe for myself the possibilities of an expert climber entering the grounds from that side. Will you take me in your boat? I'm told you have a fine one?"

"Of course I will," was the ready response. "When do you want to go?"

"As soon as you can make it convenient. I want to work rapidly, as things are coming to a focus, and I don't dare delay."

North stared at him, as if wondering how a trip in his boat would advance the work definitely, but the detective had no intention of telling him about the kidnapper's letter and, too, Wise wanted to view the whole headland from the ocean.

The result was that the two started off at once, and going first to North's bungalow to get his keys, and also his man who helped run the boat, inside of an hour Pennington Wise found himself out on the ocean with

North, and Joe Mills, who, though taciturn and even grumpy, was a good navigator.

"Remarkable cliff!" Wise exclaimed, amazed at its effect from below.

"It's all of that!" North said; "most wonderful cliff on the whole Maine coast, they say. Notice the overhang, and then tell me if any one could climb it!"

"No human being could!" Wise declared. "And I can think of no animal,—unless a spider. Go clear round to the other side, will you?"

North gave orders and Mills drove them round the great headland, and on all sides it was as massive and forbidding as the first view.

"High tide, isn't it?" asked Wise, as they went on beyond the headland, and then turned back again.

"Yes," said North, glancing at the rocky base. "Almost top notch."

"Rise high?"

"Very. Twenty feet at least."

"I thought so. Marvelous tides up in this locality. Well, there's nothing more to be discovered by gazing at these rocks and water; let's go home."

On the trip homeward, the detective proved himself so entertaining that North went back to Headland House with him.

Again they poured over the plans of the house, and Wise announced his determination of using a pick on one room in the third story that he surmised might be a trifle shorter than its adjacent walls implied.

"But it measures up," North insisted.

"Not quite," Wise declared. "There may be a two foot space in there, which would be enough for a secret passage.

"You're a persistent one!" North laughed. "All right, Mr. Wise, go ahead with your investigation. May I help? I can wield a pick with the best of them!"

The detective glanced at the lithe, sinewy form, that seemed to be all muscle and no superfluous flesh, and said, admiringly, "I believe you! But I think Kelly or the chauffeur can do the really hard work."

"No, let me do it," North offered. "I'd really enjoy it."

So, half amused at his own decision, Wise agreed, and the two went in search of the necessary tools.

But the result of their labor was absolutely nothing, beyond an incredible amount of dust and dirt, of lath and plaster, and two very much disheveled men.

"Now you must stay to dinner, Mr. North," the detective urged him. "You can put yourself to rights enough for our informal meal, and it is too late for you to get to your home by dinner time."

So North stayed, and at dinner they all discussed freely the whole affair. Mrs. Varian did not appear at the table, the nurse thinking it was better for her to have no more excitement that day.

So Zizi calmly appropriated the chair at the head of the table, and acted the part of hostess prettily and capably.

Wise changed his mind about confiding to Lawrence North the matter of the ransom letters, and concluded that in the absence of Mrs. Varian the subject might be discussed.

"At any rate," the detective summed up, "we're in the possession of positive knowledge. We know that Betty was kidnapped,—"

"Oh, come now," North said, thoughtfully, "those letters may be faked,—it seems to me they must be, —by some clever villain who expects to get all that money under false promises. I don't believe for a minute there is a kidnapper—why would anyone kidnap Betty Varian?"

"For the usual kidnapper's reason,—ransom," Wise replied.

"Well, how did the kidnapper get in?"

"Oh, Mr. North!" Wise threw up his hands. "This from you! I made up my mind that if one. more person said to me, "How did the kidnapper get in?" I'd have him arrested! I don't *know* how he got in,—but I'm going to find out!"

"I think I won't assist in the work personally the next time you try," Lawrence said. "I scarcely could get myself presentable for dinner! But, seriously, Mr. Wise, you asked me up here to consult with you. Now, I'm sure we must agree, that there is a way in and out of this house that we don't know of. And that explains the entrance of the person who killed that poor girl in the kitchen."

"And explains the disappearance of Miss Varian, and the scattering of her beads."

"Beads?" said Lawrence North, interrogatively.

"Yes; there were several beads found in the kitchen that have been identified as hers."

"Then the way in must be connected with the kitchen," North remarked.

"Perhaps, but not necessarily."

"It's a dark night, Mr. North," Rodney Granniss said, hospitably. "Won't you spend the night here? We can give you a room."

After a polite demurrer, North accepted the invitation.

The evening was spent in further and repeated discussion of the known facts and the surmised possibilities of the mystery, and then, both the detective and Granniss went about locking up the house against further marauders, and they all retired.

And the next morning they found that Lawrence North had disappeared! His room showed signs of a struggle. A chair was overturned, a rug awry and deep scratches on the shining floor proved a scuffle of some sort.

"Another kidnapping case!" Granniss exclaimed. "Must have been a husky chap that got the better of North! Could there have been two against him? He's a powerful fighter!"

"Search the house," said Wise, briefly, "and keep everybody out of North's bedroom. I'll lock it and take the key myself. Now look for him. Is he given to practical joking?"

But no amount of searching disclosed Lawrence North, or any sign of him, dead or alive. And the locked doors and windows were undisturbed.

"He certainly didn't leave of his own accord," said Granniss; "he couldn't have locked the doors behind him."

"He was carried off," cried Minna, "just as Betty was! Oh, who of us is safe now?"

CHAPTER 13: WHERE IS NORTH?

PENNINGTON WISE was at his wits' end. His wits were of the finest type and had always stood him in good stead; but he had reached their limit, at least regarding this present case.

Baffling was too mild a word for it. Uncanny it was not, for there was no hint or evidence of anything supernatural in the taking off of Lawrence North. He was a big, strong personality, and he had gone out of that house by natural means, whether voluntarily or not.

That is, of course, if he had gone out of the house. Wise was inclined to think he had, but Rodney Granniss still held to the possibility of some concealed room,—perhaps a dungeon, where the mysterious disappearances could be compassed.

Wise paid no attention to Granniss' opinions, not from any ill will toward the young man, but because he had concluded to his own satisfaction that there was really no space for a concealed room in the house.

North had come up there for the purpose of helping him look for such a matter, and North had agreed that it could not be.

And now North himself was gone,—carried off,—yet the mere phrase, "carried off" seemed to Wise incongruous.

Could North have been carried off without making noise enough to rouse some of the sleeping household? It was incredible!

Before discussing the matter with Minna, or calling the local police again, Wise went to the bedroom North had occupied and locked himself in.

"If I can't tell," he said to himself, "whether that man was kidnapped or whether he sneaked himself off—yet why would he do such a thing as that? My desperation over this puzzle is leading my mind astray."

Carefully, without touching a thing, Wise considered the state of the room.

The bed had been occupied, and, it was quite evident, had been hastily quitted. The coverings were tossed back over the footboard, and the pillow still bore the impress of a head.

On the dresser lay North's collar and tie, and beneath the pillow, Wise discovered his watch and a handkerchief.

Clearly, the man had gone, after a hasty and incomplete toilette.

On the small table, lay some sheets of paper and a pencil.

These papers were some that they had used the night before drawing plans and making measurements of the house.

Scanning the papers, Wise was startled to see a scrawled message on the corner of a sheet . It read:

They've got me. L. N.

It had been so hastily jotted down as to be almost illegible.

Had North managed to scribble it while his captor or captors looked another way? It was all too unbelievable!

The thought would creep in that North was implicated in the mystery himself. Yet that was quite as unbelievable as the rest of it,—if not more so. Wise turned his attention to the disordered furniture.

The overturned chair was not broken, but a glass tumbler was. Evidently it had been knocked off the night stand. The rug was in wrinkles and one window curtain had been partly pulled from its rod.

The scratches on the hardwood floor were apparently made by scuffling feet, but of that Wise could not be sure.

In fine, the whole disorder of the room could have been made by struggling men, or could have been faked by any one desiring to produce that effect.

"Yet I've no reason to think North faked it," Wise told himself frankly, "except that that would be an easy way out of it for me! And that message he left looks genuine,—and his watch is a valuable one,—oh, Lord, I am up against it!"

He went downstairs, and learned that Lawrence North's straw hat still hung on the hall rack. The man must have been forcibly carried off. He couldn't have walked out without collar, tie or hat! Moreover, the doors were all locked.

It still was necessary to assume a secret exit from the house.

Wise inclined to the hinged door frame, or window frame, but his most careful search failed to reveal any such. He determined to get an expert carpenter to look over the house, feeling that such would be better than an architect.

Crestfallen, dispirited and utterly nonplussed, Wise sat down in the library to think it over. First, the authorities must be told of North's disappearance, and all that, but those things he left to Granniss. The mystery was his province.

Acting on a sudden impulse, Wise started off at once for North's home. This was a good looking bungalow, of artistic effects and quiet unpretentious charm.

His knock brought the grumpy Joe Mills to the door.

"Whatcha want?" was his surly greeting.

"As I'm here on an important matter, I'll come inside," Wise said, and entered the little living room.

"Whatcha doin' here?" Mills continued. "Where's Mr. North?"

"I don't know where he is. Isn't he here?"

"Why no,—he stayed up to Headland House last night. Ain't you the detective from there?"

"Yes, I am. And Mr. North left Headland House, — er,—before breakfast this morning. Didn't he come home?"

"No, he didn't. Leastways, I ain't seen him. An' I've got work to do,—so you can leave as soon as you like."

"Look here, my man, keep a civil tongue in your head. Mr. North has disappeared, "

"Well, he's got a right to disappear if he likes,—ain't he?"

"But he went off—"

"I don't care how he went off. It's nothin' to me. An' I've got my work to do. Now you vamoose."

"Not yet," said Wise coolly, and began to look about the house. "There's no use in taking that attitude, Mr. Mills, the authorities of the village and of the county will be here shortly,—unless Mr. North turns up, which I don't think he will. Now, I'm going to do a little looking about on my own."

Wise set to work, and went swiftly over the house, from room to room. He found nothing that gave him any clue to North's disappearance nor anything that gave him much information as to North's private life.

Even an examination of the letters and notes in the small desk showed only some bills, some invitations, some circulars, that meant nothing to the detective.

He noted some memoranda in Lawrence North's handwriting and saw that it corresponded with the note left for him.

Sheriff Potter came in while he was there, but the conversation between the two men was of little interest to either.

It was all so hopeless, it seemed to Wise,—and, so blankly mysterious it seemed to Potter.

Claire Blackwood came over from her home, and Wise turned to her as to a friend.

"Do tell me something about this man, North, Mrs. Blackwood," he said. "Have you known him long?"

"Only through this summer," she replied. "He's a New Yorker, but I don't know much else about him."

"What's his business?"

"I'm not sure, but I think he's a real estate man. He's spending two months here, and he rented this bungalow furnished. You see, Mr. Wise, the people of this colony are a sort of lawless, happy go lucky set. I mean if we like any one, we don't bother to inquire into their antecedents or their social standing."

"Is North married?"

"I don't think so. At least, I've always thought him a bachelor, though nowadays you never can tell. He may have a wife, for all I know."

"At any rate, Mrs. Blackwood, he has most mysteriously disappeared. And I do hope if you know anything—anything at all, about the man, you will tell me. For, I don't mind admitting I am greatly distressed and disturbed at this new development of the Varian case."

"You connect Mr. North's disappearance with Betty Varian's, then?"

"How can I help it? Both vanished from the same house. It proves, of course, that there is a secret exit, but it is strange that such cannot be found."

"It is disappointing, Mr. Wise, to find that such a famous detective as you cannot find a concealed entrance to a country house!"

"You are not more disappointed than I am, at that fact, Mrs. Blackwood. I am chagrined, of course, but I am more frankly puzzled. The whole case is so amazing, the evidence so scanty,—clues are non existent,—what can I do? I feel like saying I was called in too late,—yet, I'm not sure I could have done better had I been here at first. I can't see where evidence has been destroyed or clues lost. It is all inexplicable."

"You are delightfully candid and far from bumptious," she said, smiling at him. "I feared you were of the know it all variety, and I see you aren't."

"Help me to know it all, Mrs. Blackwood," Wise urged. "I can't help feeling you know more about Lawrence North than any one else up here. If so, can't you tell me something of his life?"

"No, truly, Mr. Wise, I don't know any more than I've told you. He was up here last year,—this is my first season. But I don't know of any one up here now, that knows him very well. He is a quiet, reserved sort of man,—and,—as a matter of fact, we are not a gossipy lot."

Disheartened and disappointed, Wise went back to Headland House only to find that Doctor Varian had arrived during his absence.

The detective was glad to have him to talk to, for it promised at least a fresh viewpoint to be considered.

"I admit, Doctor Varian," Wise said frankly, as the two confabbed in the Varian library, "I have no theory that will fit this case at all. I have solved many mysteries, I have found many criminals, but never before have I struck a case so absolutely devoid of even an imaginary solution. Granting a criminal that desired to bring disaster to the Varian family, why should he want to abduct Lawrence North?"

"Perhaps North knew something incriminating to him," suggested the doctor.

"But that's purely supposition, there's no fact to prove it, or anything like it. As a start, suppose we assume a kidnapper of Betty Varian. Although, even before that, we have to assume a secret entrance into this house."

"That, I think, we must assume," said Varian.

"It seems so,—yet, if you knew how hard I've hunted for one! Well, then, assume a kidnapper, who, for the sake of ransom, abducts Betty Varian,—"

"And kills her father?"

"And kills her father, who interrupted the abduction."

"Good enough, so far, but what about North?"

"I can't fit North in,—unless he is in league with the criminal."

"That's too absurd. He and my brother weren't even acquaintances."

"Oh, I know it's absurd! But, what isn't? I can't see a ray of light! And, then, there's that awful matter of the maid, Martha!"

"I think, Mr. Wise, that since you admit failure, there is nothing for it, but to take Mrs. Varian away and give up the case."

"Leaving Betty to her fate!"

"We can search for the child just as well from Boston or New York as from here."

"I don't think so, Doctor. Take Mrs. Varian away, if you wish,—and if she will go. I shall stay here and solve this mystery. Because I have failed thus far, is no proof I shall continue to be unsuccessful. Mrs. Varian is a rich woman,—I am not a poor man. I shall use such funds as she provides, supplementing them, if necessary, with my own, but I shall find Betty Varian, if she's alive,—I shall find Lawrence North,—if he is alive,—and I shall discover the murderer or murderers of Frederick Varian and of Martha."

"You speak confidently, Mr. Wise."

"I do; because I mean to devote my whole soul to this thing. I can't fail, ultimately,—I *can't!*"

The man was so desperate in his determination, so sincere in his intent, that Doctor Varian was impressed, and said heartily, "I believe you will. Now, here's something I've found out. I've talked with my brother's lawyer, and I find there was something in Frederick's life that he kept secret. I don't for one minute believe it was anything disgraceful or dishonorable, for I knew my brother too well for that. But it may have been some misfortune,—or even some youthful error,—but whatever it was, it had an effect on his later years. And, there's that strange matter of the Varian pearls. Those pearls, Mr. Wise, are historic. They have never been bequeathed to any one save the oldest son or daughter of a Varian. Now, the fact that Betty and her father sometimes squabbled, is not enough to make my brother leave them to my daughter instead of to his own. Yet I can form no theory to explain the fact that he did do so. I've tried to think he was temporarily or hypochondriacally insane, but I can't reconcile that belief with my knowledge of his physical health and well being. Then, I've wondered if he ever did me a wrong in the past, that I never learned of, and if this was by way of reparation. But that is too unlikely. Again, I've thought that there might be some error in the family records, and that I might be the elder son instead of Fred. But I checked it all up, and he was two years my senior. Yet, he told the lawyer, who drew up his will, that justice demanded that the pearls be left to his niece instead of to his daughter. Now, what could he have meant by that?"

"I can't imagine, but I'm glad you have told me these things. For it makes me feel there must be something pretty serious back of all this. You don't think it could in any way reflect on Mrs. Varian?"

"No, I don't. I've talked it over with the lawyer and also with my wife, and we all agree that Minna Varian is a true, sincere and good woman. There is not only no blame or stigma to be attached to her in any way, but whatever was the secret of my brother's life, his wife knows nothing of it."

"Yet I can imagine no secret, no incident that would necessitate that strange bequest of the family pearls."

"Nor can I, except that he might have thought he owed me some reparation for some real or fancied wrong. It must have been to me, for he couldn't have wronged my daughter in any way. There was no question about the division of my father's fortune. We were the only children and it was equally shared. The pearls were Frederick's as he was the oldest child. That's all there is to the matter,—only it is strange that my brother spoke in the way he did to his lawyer. He seemed really broken up over the business, the lawyer said. And he was deeply moved when he dictated the clause leaving the pearls to Eleanor."

"Betty is really the child of the Frederick Varians?" Wise asked.

"Oh, yes. Mrs. Varian lost her first two babies in infancy, and when the third child was expected, we were all afraid it would not live. But Betty was a healthy baby from the first, and I've known her all her life."

"Her father was as fond of her as her mother was?"

"Yes,—and no. I can't explain it, Mr. Wise, but in my medical practice, I've not infrequently found a definite antipathy between a father and a daughter. For no apparent reason, I mean. Well, that condition existed between Frederick Varian and his child. They almost never agreed in their tastes or opinions, and while they were affectionate at times, yet there was friction at other times. Now, Minna and Betty were always congenial, thought alike on all subjects and never had any little squabbles. I'm telling you this in hopes it will help you, though I confess I don't see how it can."

"I hope it may,—and at any rate, it is interesting, in view of the strange occurrences up here. You've found no papers or letters bearing on this matter among Mr. Varian's effects?"

"No; except a few proofs that he was more or less blackmailed."

"And you can't learn by whom?"

"No; there were one or two veiled threats, that might have meant blackmail, and yet might not. I have them safe, but I didn't bring them up here."

"It doesn't matter, such a careful blackmailer as the one we have to deal with, never would write letters that could be traced."

"And what is to be done in this North matter?"

"First of all, I shall offer a large reward for any word of him. I have faith in offered rewards, if they are large enough. They often tempt accomplices to turn state's evidence. I've already ordered posters and advertisements with portraits of North. My agents will attend to this, and though it may bring no results, yet if it doesn't,—it will be a hint in another direction."

"Meaning?"

"That Lawrence North is implicated in the crimes."

"No, I can't agree to that. Why the man himself was carried off—"

"I know,—oh, well, Doctor Varian, first of all, we must find that secret passage. There is one,—we can't blink that fact. Now, where is it? Think of having a given problem like that, and being unable to solve it! I am so amazed at my own helplessness that I am too stunned to work!"

"Go to it, man,—you'll find it. Tear the house down, if necessary, but get at it somehow."

"I shall; I've already sent for carpenters to demolish some parts of the house."

"I wish I could stay up here and see the work progress. You'll have to find the secret, you know. You can't help it, if you tear down the whole structure."

"I don't mean to do that. I want to continue to live in the house. But some expert carpenters can dig into certain portions of it without making the rest uninhabitable, and that's what I propose doing."

"What about finger prints? I thought you detectives set great store by those."

"Not in a case like this. Suppose we find finger prints,—they're not likely to be those of any registered criminal. And since this talk with you, I shall turn my investigations in a slightly different channel, anyhow. I must look up Mr. Varian's past life—"

"Look all you wish, but I tell you now, you'll find nothing indicative. Whatever secret my brother had, it was not a matter of crime,—or even of lighter wrongdoing. And, if Frederick Varian wanted to keep the matter secret neither you nor any other detective will ever find it out!"

"That may have been true during your brother's life, Doctor, but now that he can't longer protect his secret, it must come out."

"All right, Mr. Wise, I truly hope it will For even if it reflects against my brother's integrity, it may aid in finding Betty. I don't believe that girl is dead,—do you?"

"No; I don't. I believe these letters from the kidnappers are true bills. I believe they have her concealed and confined, and by Heaven, Doctor Varian, I'm going to find her! I know that sounds like mere bluster, but I've never totally failed on a case yet,—and this,—the biggest one I've ever tackled, shall not be my first failure! I *must* succeed!"

"If I can help in any way, command me. I'm glad to see you don't think I'm criminally implicated because of the legacy of the pearls. Eleanor shall never touch them until we've positively concluded that Betty is dead. But that's a small matter. Those pearls have lain undisturbed in safe deposit many years,—they may lie there many years more,—but let the search work go on steadily."

"You know nothing of North, personally?"

"No; I never met him. Has he no relatives?"

"Haven't found any yet. But you see, the police don't hold that it is a criminal case as yet. They say he may have walked out of his own accord."

"Half dressed, and leaving his watch behind him?"

"And that note to say what had happened! That note rings true, Doctor, and either it is sincere, or North is one of the cleverest scamps I ever met up with!"

"It's conceivable that he is a scamp, but I can't see anything that points to it. Why should a perfect stranger to the Varian family cut up such a trick as to come up here and pretend to be kidnapped,—if he wasn't? It's too absurd."

"Everything is too absurd," said Wise, bitterly.

CHAPTER 14: A GREEN STAIN

TELL me more about Betty," Zizi said, "that is, if you don't mind talking about her."

"Oh, no," Minna returned, "I love to talk about her. It's the only way I can keep my hope alive!"

Zizi was sitting with Mrs. Varian while the nurse went out for a walk. There was a mutual attraction between the two, and the sympathetic dark eyes of the girl rested kindly on the face of the bereaved and suffering mother.

"Tell me about her when she was little. Was she born in New York?"

"No; at the time of her birth, we chanced to be spending a summer up in Vermont,—up in the Green Mountains. I hoped to get home before Betty arrived, but I didn't, and she was born in a tiny little hospital way up in a Vermont village. However, she was a strong, healthy baby, and has never been ill a day in her life."

"And she is so pretty and sweet,—I know not only from her picture, but from everything I hear about her. I'm going to find her, Mrs. Varian!"

Zizi's strange little face glowed with determination and she smiled hopefully.

"I don't doubt your wish to do so, Zizi, dear, but I can't think you will succeed. I'm so disappointed in Mr. Wise's failure—"

"He hasn't failed!" Zizi cried, instantly eager to defend her master. "Don't say that,—he is baffled,—it's a most extraordinary case, but he hasn't failed, —and he won't fail!"

"But he's been here a week, and what has he done so far?"

"I'll tell you what he's done, Mrs. Varian." Zizi spoke seriously. "We were talking it over this morning, and he's done this much. He's discovered, at least to his own conviction, that Betty was really kidnapped. That those letters you have received are from the abductors and that through them we must hope to trace Betty's present whereabouts. This would not be accomplished by merely following their instructions as to throwing money over the cliff. As you know, Doctor Varian advises strongly against that,—and Mr. Wise does, too. But they have learned of some more letters found among your husband's papers, signed 'Step,' and we hope to prove a connection between those and the kidnapper's letters."

"What good will that do?" Minna asked, listlessly. "Oh, Zizi, you're a dear girl, but you've no idea what I'm suffering. Nights, as I lie awake in the darkness, I seem to hear my baby Betty calling to me,—I seem to feel her little arms round my neck—somehow my mind goes back to her baby days, more than to her later years."

"That's natural, dear, when you're so anxious and worried about her. But, truly, I believe we'll get her yet. You see, everything points to the theory that she is alive."

"I'm so tired of theories,—they don't help any."

"Oh, yes, they do, dear. Now, try to get up a little more hope. Take it from me,—you'll see Betty again! She'll come dancing in, just as she used to do,—say, Mrs. Varian, why did she and her father squabble so?"

"I can't explain it. I've thought over it often, but it seems to me there was no reason for it. He admired Betty, he was proud of her beauty and grace and accomplishments, but there was something in the child that he didn't like. I hate to say this, but he seemed to have a natural dislike toward her that he honestly tried to overcome, but he utterly failed in the attempt."

"How very strange!"

"It surely is. I've never mentioned it to any one before, but you are so sympathetic, I want to ask you what you think could have been the reason for anything like that?"

"Did Betty feel that way toward him?"

"Oh, no! I mean, not naturally so. But when he would fly at her and scold her for some little, simple thing, of course she flared up and talked back at him. It was only petty bickering, but it was so frequent."

"Wasn't Mr. Varian pleased when he learned that you expected another child?"

"Yes, he was delighted. He feared it might not live,—as the others hadn't, but he was pleased beyond words at the prospect, and we both hoped for a healthy baby. He was so careful of me,—so devoted and loving, and so joyful in the anticipation of the new baby."

"He was with you in Vermont?"

"Oh, yes; we had a cottage, and he stayed there while I was in the hospital during my confinement. The house was near by, and he could come to see me at any time."

"Well, I can't understand his turning against her later. Do they look alike?"

"No,—that is, they have similar coloring, but no real resemblance."

"Betty doesn't look like you, either?"

"Not specially. Though I can't see resemblances as some people do. She was—"

"*Is*, Mrs. Varian!"

"Well, then, Betty is a dear, pretty, sweet faced girl, healthy and happy, but not remarkable in any way."

"Did she inherit your disposition or her father's?"

"Neither particularly. But I don't think a young girl often shows definite or strong traits of character."

"Some do," Zizi said, thoughtfully. "How about talents? I want to find out, you see, more of what Betty is like."

"She has a little musical talent, a taste for drawing, and a fondness for outdoor sports,—but none of these is marked. I can't describe the child otherwise than as a natural, normal everyday girl. I adore her, of course, but I am not blind to the fact that she is not a genius in any way."

"Nor do you want her to be! As you've told me of her, she seems to me a darling, and I mean to find her for you,—and for Mr. Granniss."

"Yes, Rodney loves her, and he is as desolate as I am at her loss. Oh, Zizi, have you really any hope, or are you just saying this to comfort me?"

"I really have hope, and more, I have conviction that we will yet have Betty back here. But it is not yet a certainty, and I only can offer you my own opinions. Still, dear, it's better to hope than to despair, and any day may bring us good news."

Zizi recounted this whole conversation to Pennington Wise, not so much because she deemed it important, as that he wanted every word she could get, reported to him.

The man was frankly bewildered.

"It's too ridiculous," he exclaimed to Zizi, "that I, Pennington Wise, should have a great, a unique mystery, as this one is,—and not be able to make one step of progress toward its solution!"

"'Step,'" Zizi said, "makes me think of that black mailing person, Stephen, or whatever his name is. Let's work from that end."

"I've tried and there's no place to start from. You see, the letters signed 'Step' are as untraceable as the kidnappers' letters. They're typed, not on the same machine, but on some equally obscure and unavailable one. It's impossible to hunt a typewriter, with no suspect and no indication where to look!"

"It would be for an ordinary detective, Penny, but for you—"

"That's just it, Ziz. An ordinary detective would say, 'pooh, of course we can trace that!' But I'm not an ordinary detective, and my very knowledge and experience prove to me how baffling,—how hopeless—this search is. Sometimes I think Frederick Varian did away with Betty."

"That's rubbish!" Zizi said, calmly. "But I do think there was some definite reason for Mr. Varian's attitude toward his daughter."

"No question of her paternity?"

"Good Lord, no! Minna Varian is the best and sweetest woman in the world! But I've a glimmer of a notion that I can't work out yet,—"

"Tell me."

"It's too vague to put into words." Zizi knit her heavy eyebrows, and screwed up her red lips.

And then the carpenters came, and the demolition of Headland House began. It was carefully managed; no rooms that the family used were put in disorder, but the kitchen quarters, and the cellar were desperately dug into.

"The kitchen is indicated," Wise said to Doctor Varian. "For it is clear to my mind that Betty was carried out through it."

"Through the kitchen?"

"Yes; you see, Doctor, we must reconstruct the matter like this. Betty came back to the house alone. She came in the front door with her father's key. Now, she must have been attacked or kidnapped then and there. I mean whoever did it,—and we have to assume somebody did do it,—was in the house waiting. Well—say he was,—for the moment. Then, say Betty put up a fight, which of course she would, then she was carried off through the kitchen by means of the secret passage, which we have got to find! She had the yellow pillow in her hands for some reason,—can't say what—and she dropped it on the kitchen floor,—or maybe the villain used the pillow to stifle the girl's screams."

"Go on," said Doctor Varian, briefly.

"Then, owing to the girl's struggles, the string of beads round her neck broke, and scattered over the floor."

"Only part of them."

"Yes; the others stayed with her, or were picked up by the kidnappers."

"More than one?"

"I think two. For, when Mr. Varian arrived upon the scene, one of them turned on him,—and killed him,—while there must have been another to hold Betty. It is possible there was only one, but I doubt it."

"And you think the concealed entrance is through the kitchen?"

"That, or the cellar. Anyway, there is one, and it must be found! It was used the night Martha was killed,—it was used the night North disappeared,—why, man, it *must* be there,—and I *must* find it!"

"True enough, and I hope you will."

"Here's something, Penny," Zizi said, appearing suddenly at his elbow. "I've found a stain on my frock that's exactly like the one we noticed on poor Martha's hand."

"What?"

"Yes, a green stain,—a long swish, as of green paint,—but it isn't paint."

Zizi held up a little linen frock that she sometimes wore mornings.

On the side, down near the hem, was a green smear, and it was similar in appearance to the strange mark on the hand of the dead girl.

"Where'd it come from?" asked Wise, shortly.

"I don't know, but it's the dress I wore when I was exploring the cellar, and it got pretty dirty."

"Been washed?"

"No, I shook off and brushed off most of the dirt, but this stain stuck, and wouldn't brush off. That's how I noticed it."

"Coincidence, I'm afraid. Or maybe Martha went down cellar that night for something."

"But what in the cellar would make a mark like that?"

"Dunno, Ziz. There's no green paint down there."

"It isn't paint, Penny," Zizi persisted. "It doesn't smell like paint."

"What does it smell like?"

"There's no odor to it, that I can notice. But it's a clue."

"So's the yellow pillow,—so are the scattered beads,—so was the footprint of cellar dust on the library floor,—but they're all blind clues,—they lead nowhere."

"Penny Wise! what ails you? I never knew you so ready to lie down on a job!"

"No, Zizi, not that. It's only that I can see how futile and useless all these clues are. We've got to get some bigger evidence. In fact, we can do nothing till we find the way the criminal got in and out of this house. Don't tease me, Zizi, I never was so put about!"

"You must be, when you revert to your old fashioned phrases!" the girl laughed at him, but there was deepest sympathy in her dark eyes, and an affectionate, brooding glance told of her anxiety for him.

Yet the carpenters found nothing. They proved beyond all possible doubt that there was no secret passage between the interior of Headland House and the outer world,—that there could be none, for every inch of space was investigated and accounted for.

"There's no way to get into that house except through its two doors or its windows," the master carpenter declared, and the men who were watching knew he spoke the truth.

"It proves," Granniss said, looking up from the plans to the actual walls, "it's all just as this drawing shows it."

"It certainly is," agreed Doctor Varian. "There's no missing bit."

"No," said Wise, thoughtfully, "there isn't. And, at least, the carpenters have proved that there is no secret passage built into this house. Yet there is one. I will find it."

For the first time, his words seemed to be spoken with his own conviction of their truth. His voice had a new ring,—his eyes a new brightness, and he seemed suddenly alert and powerful mentally, where, before, his hearers had thought him lacking in energy.

"You've thought of a new way to go about it?" asked Granniss.

"I have! It may not work, but I've a new idea, at least. Zizi, let me see that stained dress of yours again."

Obediently Zizi brought her frock with the smear still on its hem. Wise looked at it closely, sniffed it carefully, and gave it back, saying:

"If you want to remove that stain, dear, just wash it with soap and water. It'll come off then. Now, I'm going down to the village, and I may not be back for luncheon. Don't wait for me."

He went off, and Doctor Varian said to Zizi:

"Do you think he really has a new theory, or is he just stalling for time?"

"Oh, he's off on a new tack," she said, and her eyes shone. "I know him so well, you see, I'm sure he has a new idea and a good one. I've never seen him so cast down and so baffled as he has been over this case,—but now that his whole demeanor is changed, he has a fresh start, I know, and he'll win out yet! I never doubted his success from the beginning,—but the last two days he has been at the lowest ebb of his resources."

"I have to go back to Boston this afternoon," Doctor Varian went on, "but I'll be up again in a few days. Meantime, keep me informed, Rodney, of anything new that transpires."

Down in the little village of Headland Harbor, Pennington Wise went first to see Claire Blackwood. She seemed to know more about Lawrence North than any one else did, yet even she knew next to nothing.

"No," she told the detective, "the police haven't found out anything definite about him yet. Why don't you take up the search for him, Mr. Wise?"

"I've all I can do searching for Betty Varian," he returned with a rueful smile. "I'm not employed to hunt up North, and I am to find Miss Varian. But surely the police can get on the track of him,—a man like that can't drop out of existence."

"That's just what he's done, though," said Claire. "Do you know, Mr. Wise, I believe Lawrence North is a bigger man than we supposed. I mean a more important one, than he himself admitted. I think he was up here incognito."

"You mean that North is not his real name?"

"I don't know about that, but I mean that he wanted a rest or wanted to get away from everybody who knew him,—and so he came up here to be by himself. How else explain the fact that they can't find out anything about him?"

"Don't they know his city address?"

"Yes, but only an office,—which is closed up for the summer."

"Ridiculous! They ought to find him all the more easily if he is a man of importance."

"I don't mean of public importance, but I think—oh, I don't know what! But I'm sure there's something mysterious about him."

"I'm sure of that, too! And you know nothing of his private life, Mrs. Blackwood?"

"No; I've heard that he is a widower, but nobody seems quite certain. As I told you, up here, nobody questions one's neighbors."

"Isn't it necessary, before members are taken into the club?"

"Oh, yes; but Mr. North wasn't a member of the club. Lots of the summer people aren't members but they use the clubhouse and nobody makes much difference between members and non members. It isn't like the more fashionable beaches or resorts. We're a bit primitive up here."

"Well, tell me of North's financial standing. He's a rich man?"

"Not that I know of. But he always has enough to do what he likes. Nobody is very rich up here, yet nobody is really poor. We're a medium sized lot, in every way."

"Yet North owns a fine motor boat."

"About the best and fastest up here. But he doesn't own it, he rents it by the season. Most people do that."

"I see. And that not very pleasant factotum of his,— Joe Mills,—is he a native product?"

"No, he came up with Mr. North. He's grumpy, I admit, but he's a good sort after all. And devoted to his master."

"Ah, then he must be inconsolable at North's disappearance."

"No; on the contrary he takes it calmly enough. He says North knows his own business, and will come back when he gets ready."

"Then he knows where North is—"

"He pretends he does," corrected Claire. "I'm not sure that he is as easy about the matter as he pretends. I saw him this morning and I think he is pretty well disturbed about it all."

"Guess I'll go to see him. Thank you, Mrs. Blackwood, for your patience and courtesy in answering my questions."

"Then, Mr. Wise, if you're really grateful, do tell me what you think about the Varian affair. That's much more mysterious and much more important than the matter of Lawrence North's disappearance. Are they connected?"

"It looks so,—doesn't it?"

"Yes,—but that's no answer. Do you think they are?"

"I do, Mrs. Blackwood,—I surely do."

And Pennington Wise walked briskly over to the bungalow of Lawrence North.

He found Mills in no kindly mood.

"Whatcha want now?" was his greeting, and his scowl pointed his words.

"I want you to take me out for a sail in Mr. North's motor boat."

"Well, you gotcha nerve with you! What makes you think I'll do that?"

"Because it's for your own best interests to do so."

Wise looked the man straight in the eye, and had the satisfaction of seeing Mills' own gaze waver.

"Whatcha mean by that?" he growled, truculently.

"That if you don't take me, I'll think you have some reason for refusing."

"I gotta work."

"Your work will keep. We'll be gone only a few hours at most. How is the tide now?"

"Plumb low."

"Come on, then. We start at once."

Whether Mills decided it was best for him to consent to the trip or whether he was cowed by the detective's stern manner, Wise didn't know and didn't care, but the trip was made.

Wise directed the course, and Mills obeyed. Few words were spoken save those necessary for information.

Their course lay out around the headland, and into the small bay on the other side of it.

As they rounded the cliff, Wise directed the other to keep as close to the shore as possible.

"Dangerous rocks," Mills said, briefly.

"Steer clear of them," said Wise, sternly.

After passing round the headland on all its exposed sides, Wise declared himself ready to return.

In silence Mills turned his craft about and again Wise told him to make the trip as close to the rocky cliff as he could manage.

"You want to get us into trouble?" asked Mills, as he made a quick turn between two treacherous looking points of rock. "I nearly struck then!"

"Well, you didn't," said Wise, cheerfully.

"You're a clever sailor, Mills. Get along back home, now."

CHAPTER 15: CRIMINAL OR VICTIM?

PENNINGTON WISE came to the conclusion that he had now on hand the hardest job of his life. This knowledge did not discourage him, on the contrary it spurred him to continuous and desperate effort.

Yet, as he told Zizi, his efforts consisted mostly in making inquiries here and there, in a hope that he might learn something indicative.

"It isn't a case for clues, evidence or deduction," he told her. "It's,—I hate the word,—but it's psychological."

"If you can't be logical be psychological," said Zizi, flippantly. "Now, you know, Penny, you're going to win out "

"If I do, it'll be solely and merely because of your faith in me," he said, his face beginning to show the look of discouragement that she had learned to dread.

"That's all right," she responded, "but this old faith of mine, while it will never wear out,—it's effect on you will. Don't depend on it too long. Now let's count up what we've really got toward a solution."

"We've got a lot," began Wise hopefully. "We know enough to assume that Betty Varian was kidnapped and her father shot by the same hand. Or rather by orders of the same master brain. I don't say the criminal himself committed these crimes. Then, we know that our master villain got in and out of this house,—or his subordinates did,—by means which we haven't yet discovered, but which I am on the trail of."

"Oh, Penny, are you? Tell me where you think it is? Is it through the kitchen?"

"Wait a couple of days, Ziz. I'll tell you as soon as I'm certain. In fact, I may have to wait a week to find out about it."

"Getting an expert on it?"

"Nope. Working it out myself,—but it all depends on the moon."

"Oh, Penny, I've long suspected you of being luny, but I didn't think you'd admit it yourself! Howsumever, as long as you're jocular, I'm not discouraged. It's when you pull a long face and heave great, deep sighs that my confidence begins to wobble."

"Don't wobble yet, then, my dear, for when the moon gets around to the right quarter, I'll show you the secret way in and out of this house."

"It's too bad of you, Penny, to spring those cryptic remarks on me! Save 'em for people you want to impress with your cleverness. But all right, wait till the moon gets in apogee or perigee or wherever you want her."

"I shall. And meantime, I'm going to track down Friend North. He is a factor in the case, whether sinned against or sinning. That upset room was never upset in a real scuffle."

"It wasn't!"

"No, ma'am, it wasn't. I've been over it again, and unless I'm making the mistake of my life, that upset chair was carefully,—yes, and silently overturned by a cautious hand."

"Meaning North's?"

"Meaning North's. Of course, Ziz, I may be mistaken, so I'm not advertising this yet, but I can't see a real scuffle in that room. To begin with, if a man, or two men, or three men tried to kidnap Lawrence North and carry him off against his will don't you suppose there would be enough noise made to wake some of us?"

"Maybe they chloroformed him."

"Maybe they did. But, I'm working on a different maybe. Say that man wanted to disappear and make it look like an abduction. Wouldn't he have done just what he did do? Leave the room looking as if he had gone off unwillingly or unconsciously? The very leaving of his watch behind was a clever touch—"

"Oh, come now, Penny, I believe you *are* luny! Do you suspect Lawrence North of all the crimes? Did he abduct Betty, shoot her father,—kill Martha? and then,—finally abduct himself! And, if so,—why?"

"Zizi, you're a bright little girl, but you don't know everything. Now, you stay here and hold the fort, while I go off for a few days and stalk North. I don't say he did commit all that catalogue of crimes you string off so glibly, but I do say that he has to be accounted for,— and I must know whether he is a criminal or a victim."

Wise went away and the little family at Headland House tried to possess their souls in patience against his return.

Zizi devoted herself to the cheer and entertainment of Minna Varian, while Rodney Granniss found enough to do in looking after the accounts and financial matters of the estate.

Doctor Varian came up again, and was both surprised and pleased to find his brother's wife in such a calm, rational state of mind.

"Yet it is not a unique case," he said; "I've known other instances of hysterical and even unbalanced minds becoming rational and practical after a great shock or sorrow."

And the fearful blows Minna Varian had received from the hand of Fate, did indeed seem to change her whole nature, and instead of a pettish, spoiled woman, she was now quiet, serious, and mentally capable.

She kept herself buoyed up with a hope of Betty's return. This hope Zizi fostered, and as the days went by, it came to be a settled belief in Minna's mind, that sooner or later her child would be restored to her waiting arms.

Nurse Fletcher did not approve of this state of things at all.

"You know that girl will never be found!" she would say to Zizi. "You only pretend that you think she will, and it isn't right to fill Mrs. Varian's mind with fairy tales as you do!"

"Now, Nurse," Zizi would wheedle her, "you let me alone. I'm sure Mrs. Varian would collapse utterly if the hope of Betty's return were taken away from her. You know she would! So, don't you dare say a word that will disturb her confidence!"

Doctor Varian agreed with Zizi's ideas, regarding Minna, though he said frankly, he had grave doubts of ever seeing Betty again.

"To my mind," he said, as he and Zizi had a little confidential chat, "nothing has been accomplished. Nearly a month has passed since Betty disappeared. There is no theory compatible with a hope that she has been kept safely and comfortably all that time. The kidnappers,—if there are any—"

"Why doubt their existence?"

"Because I'm not at all sure that those ransom letters are genuine. Anybody could demand ransom."

"You're not at all sure of anything, Doctor Varian," Zizi said, "and strictly speaking, Mr. Wise isn't either. But he is sure enough to go away and stay all this time,— he's been gone ten days now, and I know unless he was on a promising trail he would have abandoned it before this."

And Pennington Wise was on a promising trail. It was proving a long, slow business, but he was making progress.

His first start had been from Lawrence North's New York office. This he found closed and locked, and no one in attendance.

Instead of being disturbed at this, he regarded it as a step forward.

The owner of the building in which Mr. North's office was, told the detective that Mr. North had gone away for the summer,—that he had said, his office would be closed until September, at least, and that there was nothing doing.

Wise persuaded him that there was a great deal doing and in the name of justice and a few other important personages he must hand over a key of that office.

At last this was done, and Wise went eagerly about the examination of Lawrence North's books and papers.

The fact that he found nothing indicative, was to him an important indication. North's business, evidently, was of a vague and sketchy character. He seemed to have an agency for two or three inconspicuous real estate firms, and he appeared to have put over a few unimportant deals.

What was important, however, was a small advertisement, almost cut out from a newspaper and almost overlooked by the detective.

This was a few lines expressing somebody's desire to rent a summer home on the seashore, preferably on the Maine coast.

It was signed F. V. and Wise thought that it might have been inserted by Frederick Varian. He hadn't heard that the Varians took Headland House through the agency of or at the suggestion of North, yet it might be so.

At any rate there was nothing else of interest to Wise in North's whole office,—and he left no paper unread or book unopened.

It took a long time, but when it was accomplished the detective set out on a definite and determined search for North.

The man proved most elusive. No one seemed to know anything about him. If ever a negligible citizen lived in these United States, it was, the detective concluded, Lawrence North.

He hunted directories and telephone books. He visited mercantile agencies and information bureaus. He had circulars already out with a reward offered for the missing man, but none of his,efforts gave the slightest success.

Had he been able to think of North as dead, he could have borne defeat better, but he envisaged that nonchalant face as laughing at his futile search!

There was, of course, the possibility that North was an assumed name, and that the true name of the man might bring about a speedy end to his quest. But this was mere surmise, and he had no way of verifying it.

By hunting down various Norths here and there, he one day came upon a woman who said,

"Why, I once knew a woman named Mrs. Lawrence North. She lived in the same apartment house I did, and I remember her because she had the same name. No, her husband was no relation of my husband,—my husband has been dead for years."

"Was her husband dead?" Wise inquired.

"No, but he better 'a' been! He only came to see her once in a coon's age. He kept her rent paid, but he hardly gave her enough money to live on! He was one of these hifalutin artistic temperament men, and he just neglected that poor thing somethin' fierce!"

"What became of her?"

"Dunno. Maybe she's livin' there yet."

To the address given Wise went, scarcely daring to hope he was on the right track at last.

At the apartment house he was informed that Mrs. Lawrence North had lived there but that she had also died there, about three months previous. The superintendent willingly gave him all the details he asked, and Pennington Wise concluded that the woman who had died there was without doubt the wife of the Lawrence North he was hunting for.

But further information of North's later history he could not gain. After the death of his wife he had given up the apartment, which was a furnished one and had never been there since.

Wise cogitated deeply over these revelations. So far, he had learned nothing greatly to North's discredit, save that he had not treated his wife very well, and that he had, directly after her death, gone to a summer resort and mingled with the society there.

Yet this latter fact was not damaging. To his knowledge, North had in no way acted, up at Headland Harbor, in any way unbecoming a widower. He had not been called upon to relate his private or personal history, and if he had sought diversion among the summer colony of artists and dilettantes, he had, of course, a right to do so.

Yet, the whole effect of the man was suspicious to Wise.

He told himself it was prejudice, that there was no real evidence against him,—that—but, he then thought, if North was a blameless, undistinguished private citizen, why, in heaven's name would anybody want to kidnap him?

This he answered to himself by saying North might have learned some secret of the kidnappers or of the secret entrance that made it imperative for the criminals to do away with him. This might also explain the death of the maid, Martha.

Yet, through it all, Wise believed that North was in wrong. How or to what extent he didn't know, but North must be found. So to the various undertakers' establishments he went until at last he found the one who had had charge of the obsequies of Mrs. Lawrence North.

That was a red letter day in the life of Pennington Wise. For, though he gained no knowledge there of his elusive quarry, he did learn the name and former dwelling place of the woman North married.

She had been, he discovered, a widow, and had been born in Vermont. Her name when she married North was Mrs. Curtis, and they had been married about ten years ago.

This, while not an astounding revelation was of interest and, at least promised a further knowledge of North's matrimonial affairs.

The town in Vermont was Greenvale, a small village Wise discovered, up in the northern part of the state.

It was a long trip, but the detective concluded that that this case on which he was engaged was a case of magnificent distances and he at once made his railroad reservations and bought his tickets.

Meantime the household at Headland House had been thrown into a new spasm of excitement by the receipt of a letter from a stranger.

It was addressed to Mrs. Varian, and was of a totally different character from the frequent missives she received telling of girls who looked like the pictures of the advertised lost one.

This was a well written, straightforward message that carried conviction by its very curtness.

It ran:

Mrs. Varian,
Dear Madam:
I address you regarding a peculiar experience I have just had. I am deaf, therefore I never go to the theatre, as I can't hear the lines. But I go often to the Moving Pictures. Of late I have been taking lessons in Lip Reading, and though I have not yet progressed very far in it, I can read lips sometimes, especially if the speaker makes an effort to form words distinctly. Now last night I went to the Movies and in a picture there was a girl, who seemed to be speaking yet there was no occasion in the story for her to do so. She was merely one of a crowd standing in a meadow or field. But as practice in my Lip Reading I watched her and I am sure she said, "I am Betty Varian,—I am Betty Varian." This seemed so strange that I went again this afternoon, and saw the picture again,— and I am sure that was what she said,—over and over. I don't know that this will interest you, but I feel I ought to tell you.
Very truly yours,
ELLA SHERIDAN.

"It can't mean anything," Minna said. "Whereever Betty is, she isn't in a moving picture company!"

"But wait a minute," cried Granniss, "when they take pictures of crowds, you know,—in a field or meadow, they pick up any passer by or any one they can get to fill in."

"Even so," Zizi said, "I can't see it. I think somebody was talking about Betty and the girl read the lips wrong. She's only a beginner, she says. I've heard it's a most difficult thing to learn."

"I don't care," Granniss said, "it's got to be looked into. I'm going to answer this letter,—no, I'm going straight down there, it's from Portland, and I'm going to see that picture myself."

"Make sure it's still being shown," said the practical Zizi.

"I'll telegraph and ask her," cried Rodney; his face alight at the thought of doing some real work himself.

"Oh, don't go, Rod," Minna said; "I can't get along without you,—and what good will it do? You know a picture isn't the real people, and—oh, it's all too vague and hazy—"

"No, it isn't," Granniss insisted. "It's the first real clue. Why didn't that girl notice what the girl in the picture looked like? Oh, of course I must go! I can get to Portland and back in three days, and—why, I've got to go!"

And go he did.

The picture was still on at the theater, and with a beating heart Rodney took his seat to watch it.

He could scarce wait for the preliminary scenes, he knew no bit of the plot or what happened to the characters: he sat tense and watchful for the appearance of the crowd on the meadow.

At last it came,—and, he nearly sprang from his seat,—it was Betty! Betty Varian herself,—he could not be mistaken! She wore a simple gingham frock, a plain straw hat, and had no sign of the smartness that always characterized Betty's clothes, but he could not be deceived in that face, that dear, lovely face of Betty herself!

And he saw her lips were moving. He could not read them, as the girl who told of it had done, but he imagined she said, "I am Betty Varian,—I am Betty Varian."

Yet her face was expressionless,—no eager air of imparting information, no apparent interest in the scene about her,—the face in the screen seemed like that of an automaton saying the words as if from a lesson.

Rod couldn't understand it. He feared that it was merely a chance likeness,—he had heard of exact doubles,—and as the scene passed, and the crowd on the meadow returned no more to the story, he left his seat and went in search of the owner of the theater.

But all his questioning failed to elicit any information as to the scene or where it was taken. The theatrical manager arranged for his picture through an agent and knew nothing of the company that took it or the author of the play.

The next morning Rodney tried again to locate the producer, but failing, decided to return home and put the matter in the hands of Pennington Wise:

He was sure the girl on the screen was Betty, yet had he been told authoritatively that it was not, he could believe himself the victim of a case of mistaken identity.

He related his experiences to Minna and Zizi and they both felt there was little to hope for as a result.

"You see," Zizi explained it, "when those crowds are picked up at random that way, they are always chatting about their own affairs. Now, it may well be this girl had been reading the circulars about Betty, also she may have been told how much she looked like her, and that would explain her speaking the name. And except for the actual name, I don't believe the Ella Sheridan person read it right."

"I don't either," Minna agreed. "I wish I could see something in it, Rod, but it's too absurd to think of Betty in the moving pictures, even by chance, as you say. And, too, where could she be that she would saunter out and join in a public picture like that?"

"I know, it seems utterly absurd,—but—it was Betty,—it was, it was! When will Mr. Wise be back, Zizi?"

"I had a letter this morning, and he says not to expect him before the end of the week at least. He is on an important trail and has to go to a distant town, then he will come back here."

"Oh, I want to consult him about this thing," and Rodney looked disconsolate.

"Work at it yourself, Rod," Zizi advised him. "Get lists of the picture making companies, write to them all, and track down that film. It must be a possible thing to do. Go to it!"

"I will," Rodney declared, and forthwith set about it.

"Now, I want to go off on a little trip," Zizi said to Minna. "And I don't want to say where I'm going, for it may turn out a wild goose chase. The idea is not a very big one,—yet it might be the means of finding out a lot of the mystery. Anyway, I want to go, and I'll be back in three days or four at most."

"I hate to have you leave me, Zizi," Mrs. Varian answered, "but if it means a chance, why take it. Get back as soon as you can, I've grown to depend on you for all my help and cheer."

So Zizi packed her bag and departed.

With her she took a letter that she had abstracted from a drawer of Minna Varian's writing desk.

She had taken it without leave, indeed without the owner's knowledge, but she felt the end justified the means.

"If indeed the end amounts to anything," Zizi thought, a little ruefully.

Once started on her journey, it seemed like a wilder goose chase than it had at first appeared.

The route, the little, ill appointed New England railroad, took her inland into the state of Maine, and then westward, until she was in the green hills and valleys of Vermont.

It was when the conductor sung out "Greenvale" that Zizi, her journey ended, alighted from the train.

She found a rickety old conveyance known as a buckboard and asked the indifferent driver thereof if she might be conveyed to any inn or hostelry that Greenvale might boast.

Still taciturn, the lanky youth that held the horse told her to "get in."

Zizi got in, and was transported to a small inn that was not half so bad as she had feared.

She paid her charioteer, and as he set her bag down for her on the porch, she went into the first room, which seemed to be the office.

"Can I have a room for a day or two?" she asked.

"Sure," said the affable clerk, looking at her with undisguised admiration.

Zizi smiled at him, quite completing his subjugation, for she wished to be friendly in order to get all the help she could on her mission.

She registered, and then said,

"Greenvale is a lovely place. How large is it?"

"'Most three thousand," said the clerk, proudly. "Gained a lot of late."

"Do you have many visitors in the summer?"

"Lots; and we've got a noted one here right now."

"Who?"

"Nobody less than—why, here he comes now!" and Zizi looked toward the door, and just entering, she saw,— Pennington Wise!

CHAPTER 16: IN GREENVALE

"FOR the love of Mike, Zizi, what are you doing here?" exclaimed Pennington Wise, nearly struck dumb with astonishment at sight of the girl.

"I ask you that!" she returned, looking at him with equal amazement.

"Well, anyway, I'm glad to see you;" he smiled at her with real pleasure. "I've had a long, horrid and most unsatisfactory quest for the elusive L. N. and I haven't found him yet."

"Any hope of it?"

"Nothing but. I mean no expectation or certainty,— but always hope. Now, what's your lay? Why,—Zizi, tell me why you're here, or I'll fly off the handle!"

"Well, wait till we can sit down somewhere and talk comfortably. I haven't had a room assigned to me yet."

"But tell me this: you're here on the Varian case?"

"Yes, of course. Are you?"

"I am. Oh, girl, there must be something doing when we're here from different starting points and for different reasons!"

"I'm here because of some revelations of Mrs. Varian," Zizi said and Wise stared at her.

"Mrs Varian!" he exclaimed. "I say, Ziz, go to your room, get your bag unpacked and your things put away as quick as you can, won't you? And then let's confab."

Zizi darted away, she arranged to have a bedroom and sitting room that she could call her own for a few days, and in less than half an hour, she was receiving Wise in her tiny but pleasant domain.

"Now," he said, "tell me your story."

"It isn't much of a story," Zizi admitted,—"but I came here because this is where Betty Varian was born."

"Up here? In Greenvale, Vermont?"

"Yes,—in a little hospital here."

"And what has that fact to do with Betty's disappearance?"

"Oh, Penny, I don't know! But I hope,—I believe it has something!"

"Well, my child, I'm up here to investigate the early life of Mrs. Lawrence North."

"Then we are most certainly brought to the same place by totally different clues,—if they are clues, and one or both of them must prove successful! Who was she, Penny?"

"As near as I can find out, she was a widow when North married her. Her name was then Mrs. Curtis. Her maiden name I don't know."

"Well, what's the procedure?"

The procedure, as Wise mapped it out, was to go to the hospital first and see what could be learned concerning Mrs. Varian's stay there twenty years ago.

They had no difficulty in getting an interview with the superintendent of the institution, but as Wise had feared, he was not the man who had been in charge a score of years previous.

In fact, there had been several changes since, and the present incumbent, one Doctor Hasbrook, showed but slight interest in his callers' questions.

"The hospital is only twenty two years old," Hasbrook said, "so the patient you're looking up must have been here soon after it was opened."

"You have the records, I suppose?" asked Wise.

"Yes,—if you care to hunt them over, they are at your disposal."

As a result of this permission, Wise and Zizi spent several hours looking over the old and not very carefully kept records of the earliest years of the little country hospital.

"The worst of it is," said Zizi, "I don't exactly know what we're hoping to find, do you?"

"I have a dim idea, Zizi, and it's getting clearer," Wise replied, speaking as from a deep absorption.

"Here's something."

"What?"

"It's a list of births for a year,—the year Betty Varian was born and,—oh, Zizi! the very same night that Mrs. Varian's baby was born, a Mrs. Curtis also bore a child!"

"Well?"

"Oh, don't sit there and babble 'What?' and 'Well?' Can't you see?"

"No, I can't."

"Well, wait a bit,—now, let me see,—yes, Miss Morton,—h'm,—Miss Black—"

"Pennington Wise, if you've lost your mind, I'll take you to a modern sanitarium,—I don't want to go off and leave you here in this little one horse hospital!"

"Hush up, Zizi, don't chatter! Miss Morton,—h'm—"

Zizi kept silent in utter exasperation. She knew Wise well enough to be sure he was on the trail of a real discovery, but her impatience could scarcely stand his mutterings and his air of suppressed excitement.

However, there was nothing to do but wait for his further elucidation and when at last he closed the books and looked up at her, his face was fairly transfigured with joyous expectancy.

"Come on, girl," he cried, "come on."

He rose, and, as Zizi followed, they went back to the superintendent's office.

"Can you tell us, Doctor Hasbrook," Wise asked, "where we can find two nurses who were here twenty years ago? One was named Black and one Morton."

This was a matter of definite record, and Hasbrook soon informed them that Nurse Black had died some years ago but that Nurse Morton had married and was still living in Greenvale."

"Thank Heaven," murmured Wise as he took the address of Mrs. Briggs, who had been Nurse Morton.

To her house they then went, Zizi now quite content to trudge along by the detective's side, without asking further questions. She knew she would learn all in due time.

The pretty little cottage which was the home of Mrs. Briggs they found and went through the wooden picket gate and up to the front door.

"Something tells me she won't be glad to see us," Wise whispered, and then they were admitted by a middle aged woman who answered Wise's courteous question by stating that she was Mrs. Briggs.

She looked amiable enough, Zizi thought, and she asked her callers to be seated in her homely but comfortable sitting room.

"I am here," Wise began, watching her face for any expression of alarm, "to ask you a few questions about some cases you attended when you were a nurse in the Greenvale Hospital."

"Yes, sir," was the non committal response, but Zizi's quick eye noticed the woman's fingers grasp tightly the corner of her apron, which she rolled and twisted nervously.

"One case, especially, was that of a Mrs. Varian. You remember it?"

"No,—I do not," Mrs. Briggs replied, but it was after a moment's hesitation, and she spoke, in a low, uncertain voice.

"Oh, yes, you do," and Wise looked at her sternly. "Mrs Frederick Varian,—a lovely lady, who gave birth to a girl child, and you were her attendant."

"No; I don't remember any Mrs. Varian." The voice was steadier now but the speaker kept her eyes averted from the detective's face.

"Your memory is defective," he said, quietly. "Do you, then, remember a Mrs. Curtis?"

This shot went home, and Mrs. Briggs cried out excitedly, "What do you mean? Who are you?"

"You haven't been asked anything about these people for twenty years, have you?" Wise went on.

"You didn't think you ever would be asked about them, did you? Your memory is all right,—now what have you to say—"

"I have nothing to say. I remember a Mrs. Curtis, but she was not my patient."

"No; Mrs. Varian was your patient. But Mrs. Curtis figured in the Varian case pretty largely, I should say!"

Mrs Briggs broke down. "I didn't do any harm," she said. "I only did what I was told. I obeyed the others who were in greater authority than I was." She buried her face in her apron and sobbed.

"That's right, Mrs. Briggs,"Wise said kindly; "tell the truth, and I promise you it will be far better for you in the long run, than to make up any falsehoods."

"Tell me what happened," the woman said, eagerly, as she wiped her eyes. "Oh, sir, tell me? Did Mrs—Mrs Varian's little girl live to grow up?"

"Mrs *Varian's* little girl!" Wise repeated with a strange intonation and a shrewd shake of his head.

"Yes, Mrs. Varian's little girl," the woman insisted obstinately. "They took the child away when it was four weeks old, Mrs. Varian was quite well and happy then."

"Of course she was,—but, were you happy?"

"Why not?" The words were defiant, but Mrs. Briggs' face showed an involuntary fear.

"Come now, Mrs. Briggs, tell me the whole story and you will get off scot free. Keep back the truth or any portion of the truth, and you will find yourself in most serious trouble. Which do you choose?"

"Where are the Varians? Where is Mr. Varian?"

"Mr Varian is dead. You have me to reckon with instead of him. Oh, I begin to see! Was it Mr. Varian's scheme?"

"Yes, it was. I told you I had no choice in the matter."

"Because he paid you well. Now, are you going to tell me, or must I drag the story from you, piecemeal?"

"I'll—I'll tell."

"Tell it all, then. Begin at the beginning."

"The beginning was merely that the Varians were spending the summer here in a little cottage over on the next street to this. Mrs. Varian was expecting a confinement but hoped to get back to the city before it took place. However, she was not well, and Mr. Varian brought her to the hospital for consultation and treatment. I was her nurse, and I came to know her well, and—to love her. She was a dear lady, and as her first babies had died in infancy she was greatly worried and anxious lest this new baby should be sickly or, worse, should be born dead.

"Mr Varian was the most devoted husband I ever saw. He put up with all his wife's whims and tantrums,—and she was full of them,—and he indulged and petted her all the time. He was quite as anxious as she for a healthy child, and when they discovered that she must remain here for her confinement, he sent to town for all sorts of things to make her comfortable and happy.

"Well,—the baby was born,—and it was born dead. Mrs. Varian did not know it, and when I told Mr. Varian, he was so disappointed I thought he would go off his head.

"Now there was another case in the hospital that was a very sad matter. It was Mrs. Curtis. She, poor woman, was confined that same night, and her baby was born, fine and healthy. But she didn't want the child. She was so poor she scarce could keep soul and body together. She had three little children already and her husband had died by accident only a month before. How to care for a new little one, she didn't know.

"It was Nurse Black who thought of the plan of substituting the lovely Curtis child for the dead Varian baby, and we proposed it to Mr. Varian. To our surprise he fairly jumped at it. He begged us to ascertain if Mrs. Curtis would agree, saying he would pay her well. Now, Mrs. Curtis was only too grateful to be assured of a good home and care for her child, and willingly gave it over to the Varians. But Mrs. Varian never knew.

"That was Mr. Varian's idea, and it was an honest and true desire to please his wife and to provide her with a healthy child such as she herself could never bear.

"I think Mr. Varian was decided at the last by the piteous cries of Mrs. Varian for her baby. When he heard her, he said quickly, "Take the Curtis child to her,—and see if she accepts it?"

"And did she?" asked Zizi, her eyes shining at the dramatic story.

"Oh, she did! She cried out in joy that it was her baby and a beautiful, healthy child, and she was so pleased and happy and contented that she dropped off into a fine, natural sleep and began to get well at once. When she wakened she asked for the child, and so it went on until there was no question what to do. The whole matter was considered settled—"

"Who knew of the fraud?" asked Wise.

"No one in the world but Mrs. Curtis, Mr. Varian and we two nurses. Mr. Varian paid the poor mother ten thousand dollars, and he gave us a thousand dollars apiece. The authorities of the hospital never knew. They assumed the dead child was Mrs. Curtis' and the living child was Mrs. Varian's

"And the doctors?"

"There was but one. I forgot him. Yes, he knew, but he was a greedy scamp, and Mr. Varian easily bought him over. He died soon after, anyway."

"So that now,—what living people know of this thing?"

"Why—you say Mr. Varian is dead?"

"Yes."

"And Mrs. Varian never learned the truth?"

"No," Zizi answered, emphatically, "she never did."

"And Nurse Black is dead, and the doctor is dead,— why, then nobody knows it—oh, yes, Mrs. Curtis, of course."

"She, too, is dead," Wise said.

"Then nobody knows it but we three here. Unless of course, Mr. Varian or Mrs. Curtis told."

"Mr Varian never did," Wise said,—"as to Mrs. Curtis I can't say."

"Oh, she'd never tell," Mrs. Briggs declared.

"She was honest in the whole matter. She said she didn't know how she'd support her three children, let alone a fourth. And, she was glad and thankful to have it brought up among rich and kind people. She never would have let it go unless she had been sure of their kindness and care, but we told her what fine people the Varians were and she was satisfied."

"Were there adoption papers taken out?" Mrs. Briggs stared at Wise's question.

"Why, no; it wasn't an adoption, it was a substitution. How could there be an adoption? Mrs. Varian thought it her own child,—the authorities of the hospital thought the living child was Mrs. Varian's. The matter was kept a perfect secret."

"And I think it was all right," Zizi defended. "So long as Mr. Varian knew, so long as Mrs. Curtis was satisfied, I don't see where any harm was done to anybody."

"I don't either, miss," said Mrs. Briggs eagerly. "I'm gratified to hear you say that, and I hope, sir, you feel the same way about it."

"Why, I scarcely know what to say," Wise returned. "It depends on whether you view the whole thing from a judicial—"

"Or from a viewpoint of common sense and kind heartedness!" Zizi said. "I think it was fine,—and I'm only sorry for poor Mr. Varian who had to bear the weight of his secret all alone through life."

"Oh, Zizi, that would explain the pearls!" Wise cried.

"Of course it does! He had to leave them to a Varian,—and Betty wasn't a Varian,—oh, Penny, what a situation! That poor man!"

"And it explains a lot of other things," Wise said, thoughtfully. "Well, Mrs. Briggs, we'll be going now. As to this matter, I think I can say, if you'll continue to keep it secret, we will do the same, at least for the present. Did you never tell anybody? Not even your husband?"

"I never did. It was the only secret I ever kept from my husband, he's dead now this seven year, poor man,— but I felt I couldn't tell him. It wasn't my secret. When I took Mr. Varian's money, I promised never to tell about the child. And I kept my word. Until now," she added, and Wise said,

"You had to tell now, Mrs. Briggs, if you hadn't told willingly and frankly, I could have brought the law to bear on your decision."

"That's what I thought, sir. Please tell me of the child? Is she now a fine girl?"

Wise realized that up in this far away hamlet the news of Betty Varian's disappearance had not become known, so he merely said,

"I've never seen her, but I'm told she is a fine and lovely girl. Her mother is a charming woman."

"I'm glad you say so, sir, for though I was sorry for her, she was a terror for peevishness and fretting. Yet, after she got the little girl she seemed transformed, she was that happy and content."

Back to the inn went Pennington Wise and Zizi.

"The most astonishing revelation I ever heard," was Wise's comment, as he closed the door of Zizi's sitting room and sat down to talk it over.

"Where do you come out?"

"At all sorts of unexpected places. Now, Zizi, have you realized yet that Lawrence North married that Mrs. Curtis?"

"You're sure?"

"Practically; he married a widow named Curtis, who formerly lived in Greenvale, Vermont. I've not struck any other. And besides, it connects North with this whole Varian case and I'm sure he is mixed up in it."

"But how?"

"That's the question. But here's a more immediate question, Zizi. Are we to tell Mrs. Varian what we have learned from the nurse up here?"

"How can we help telling her?"

"But, think, Zizi. Have we a right to divulge Frederick Varian's secret? After he spent his life keeping it quiet, shall we be justified in blurting it out—"

"Oh, Penny, that's why Mr. Varian and Betty were at odds! She wasn't his child—"

"She didn't know that—"

"No; but he did, and it made him irritable and impatient. Oh, don't you see? He was everlastingly thinking that her traits were not Varian traits nor traits of her mother's family,—and he couldn't help thinking of the child's real mother,—and oh, I can see how altogether he was upset over and over again when Betty would do or say something that he didn't approve of."

"Yes, that's so,—but Zizi, here's a more important revelation. The reason Frederick Varian was so opposed to Betty's marrying was because he found himself in such an equivocal position! He couldn't let her marry a decent man without telling him the story of her birth,—yet, he couldn't tell it! He couldn't tell the young man without telling his wife,—and to tell Mrs. Varian,—at this late date,—oh, well, no wonder the poor father,—who was no father,—was nearly distracted. No wonder he was crusty and snappish at Betty,—yet of course the poor girl was in no way to blame!"

"Wouldn't you think Mrs. Varian would have suspected?"

"No; why should she? And, too, her husband took good care that she shouldn't. It's a truly marvelous situation!"

CHAPTER 17: THE LAST LETTER

WHEN Wise and Zizi returned to Headland House, they found Doctor Varian there on one of his brief visits.

Deciding that it was the best course to pursue the detective took the physician entirely into his confidence. The two were closeted in the library, and Wise related his discoveries regarding the Vermont hospital.

"It is astounding! Incredible!" exclaimed Varian, "but if true, and it must be true, it explains a great many things. As a doctor, I can understand these things, and looking back, I see that Betty never had any traits of either parent. Not always are children like their parents but I've never seen a case where there was not some sign of heredity, some likeness to father or mother in looks or character.

"But Betty showed none such. She was a dear girl, and we all loved her,—but she was not in any way like Fred or Minna. To be sure, I never thought about this definitely, for I had no reason to think of such a thing as you're telling me. But, recollecting Betty, for I've known her all her life, I can see where she is of a totally different stamp from my brother or his wife. My, what a case!"

"Do you blame Mr. Varian?"

"Not a bit! He did it out of the kindest of motives. He was not only a devoted husband but a willing slave to his wife, even in cases where she was unreasonable or over exacting. He petted and humored her in every imaginable way, and when the third baby was expected, the poor man was nearly frantic lest it should not live and Minna could not bear the disappointment. And so, when, as it seems by a mere chance he had an opportunity to provide her with a strong, healthy, beautiful child,—I, for one, am not surprised that he did so, nor do I greatly blame him.

As you represent it, the poor mother was willing and glad to consent to the arrangement. An adoption would have been perfectly legitimate and proper. Fred only chose the substitution plan to save Minna from trouble and worry. I know Fred so well, he was impulsive and he stopped at nothing to please or comfort his wife. So, I can easily see how he decided, on the impulse of the moment, to do this thing, and if, as you say, Minna took to the child at once, and loved it as her own, of course he felt that the plan must be kept up, the deception must be maintained."

"It accounts, I dare say, for the slight friction that so frequently arose between Betty and her father,—for we may as well continue to call him her father."

"It does. I suppose when the child exhibited traits that annoyed or displeased Fred, he resented it and he couldn't help showing it. He had a strong clannish feeling about the Varians and he was sensitive to many slight faults in Betty that Minna never gave any heed to."

"It's an interesting study in the relative values of heredity and environment."

"Yes, it is; and it proves my own theory which is that their influences average about fifty fifty. Many times heredity is stronger than environment, and often it's the other way, but oftenest of all, as in this case, the one offsets the other. I know nothing of Betty's real ancestry, but it must have been fairly good, or Fred never would have taken her at all."

"And it was, of course, his clannish loyalty to his family name that would not let him leave the pearls to Betty."

"Yes, they have always been left to a Varian and Fred couldn't leave them to one who was really an outsider."

"It also explains Mr. Varian's objections to Betty's marriage."

"Oh, it does! Poor man, what he must have suffered. He was a high strung nature, impulsive and even impetuous, but of a sound, impeccable honesty that wouldn't brook a shadow of wrong to any one."

"I suppose what he had done troubled him more or less all his life."

"I suppose so. Not his conscience,—I can see how he looked on his deed as right,—but he was bothered by circumstances,—and it was a difficult situation that he had created. The more I realize it, the sorrier I feel for my poor brother. To make his will was a perplexity! His lawyer has told me that when he left the pearls away from Betty, he said, "I *must* do it! I *have* to do it!" in a voice that was fairly agonized. The lawyer couldn't understand what he meant, but assumed it was some cloud on Betty's birth. I daresay Fred was not bothered about his money, for he knew if he died first, Minna would provide for Betty. But the pearls he had to arrange for. Oh, well, Mr. Wise, now then, viewed in the light of these revelations, where do we stand? Who killed my brother? Who killed the maid, Martha? Who kidnapped Betty and Mr. North?"

"Those are not easy questions, Doctor Varian," Wise responded, with a grave face, "but of this I am confident,—one name will answer them all."

"You know the name?"

"I am not quite sure enough yet to say that I do, —but I have a strong suspicion. I think it is the man who wrote the blackmailing letters to Mr. Varian."

"The man we call Stephen? It well may be. They referred to a robbed woman. Now, my brother never robbed anybody in the commonly accepted sense of that term, but it may mean the mother of Betty. Could the doctor in the Greenvale Hospital, that attended the two women that night, be trying to make money out of the matter?"

"They tell me he died some years ago."

"But these letters are not all recent. And, too, he might have divulged the secret before he died, and whoever he told used it as a threat against my brother."

"It's hardly a blackmailing proposition."

"Oh, yes, it is. Say the doctor,—or the doctor's confidant threatened Fred with exposure of the secret of Betty's birth, I know my brother well enough to be certain that he would pay large sums before he would bring on Minna and Betty the shock and publicity, even though there was no actual disgrace."

"Well, then, granting a blackmailer, he's the one to look for, but on the other hand, why should he kill Mr. Varian, when he was his hope of financial plunder? Why should he kidnap Betty? And, above all, why should he kill Martha and abduct Lawrence North?"

"The only one of those very pertinent questions that I can answer is the one about Betty. Whoever kidnapped her, did it for ransom. That is evidenced by the letters to Minna."

"If they are genuine."

"Oh, they are,—I'm sure. She had another while you were away."

"She did! To what purport?"

"Further and more desperate insistence of the ransom,—and quickly."

"The regular procedure! If it is a fake they would do the same thing."

"Yes,—and they would also, if it is a real issue."

Wise went at once to find Minna and see the new letter.

It was indeed imperative, saying, in part:

"Now we have Betty safe, but this is your last chance to get her back. We are too smart for your wise detective and we are in dead earnest. Also Betty will be dead in earnest unless you do exactly as we herein direct. Also, this is our last letter. If you decide against us, we settle Betty's account and call the whole deal off. Our instructions are the same as before. On Friday night, at midnight, go to the edge of the cliff and throw the package of money over. Tie to it some float and we will do the rest. That is, if you act in sincerity. If you are false minded in the least detail,

we will know it. We are wiser than Wise. So take your
choice and,—have a care! No one will be more faithful
than we, if you act in good faith. Also, no one can be worse
than we can be, if you betray us!"

The somewhat lengthy letter was written on the same
typewriter as had been used for the others, and Wise
studied it.

"There's nothing to be deduced from the materials," he
said. "They're too smart to use traceable paper or typing.
But there are other indications, and, I think, Mrs. Varian,
at last I see a ray of hope, and I trust it will soon be a
bright gleam and then full sunshine!"

"Good!" Zizi cried, clapping her hands. "When Penny
talks poetry, he's in high good humor,—and when he's in
high good humor, it's 'cause he's on the right track,—and
when he's on the right track,—he gets there!"

Then they told Wise about the strange communication
from the girl who knew lip reading, and the detective was
even more highly elated.

"Great!" he exclaimed. "Perfectly remarkable! Where's
Granniss?"

"Gone to Boston to see a moving picture concern. He
may have to go on to New York. He hopes to be back by
Saturday at latest."

It was Minna who answered, and her face was
jubilant at the hope renewed in her heart by Wise's own
hopefulness.

But she determined in her secret thoughts to throw
the money over the cliff on Friday night, whether the
detective agreed to that plan or not. What, she argued to
Mrs. Fletcher, whom she took into her confidence on this
matter, was any amount of money compared to the mere
chance of getting back her child? She urged and bribed
Fletcher until she consented to help Minna get out of the
house on Friday night without Wise's knowledge.

It was now Tuesday, and after much questioning of
every one in the house as to what had taken place in his

absence, the detective shut himself alone in the library, and surrounded by his own written notes, and with many of Mr. Varian's letters and financial papers, he thought and brooded over it all for some hours.

At last he opened the door and called Zizi "Well, my child," he said, closing the door behind her, "I've got a line on things."

"I do hope, Penny, you'll watch out for Mrs. Varian. She's going to throw the money over the cliff on Friday night without your knowledge or consent."

"She can't do that."

"She can't without your knowledge, I admit. But, she can without your consent. Her money is her own and you've no real authority that will let you dictate to her how to use it."

"True, oh, Queen!"

"Oh, Penny, when you smile like that, I know something's up! What is it?"

"My luck, I hope. Ziz, do you remember you said you had a green smear on your frock like the one on Martha's hand?"

"Yes; why?"

"Is it there yet, or did you clean it off?

"It's there yet, I haven't worn the dress since."

"Get it, will you?"

Zizi went, and returned with the little frock, a mere wisp of light, thin material, and handed it to Pennington Wise.

He inspected the green streak, which was visible though not conspicuous, and then he sniffed at it with such absorption that Zizi laughed outright.

"Pen," she said, "in detective stories they always represent the great detective as sniffing like a hound on a scent. You're literally doing it."

"Not astonishing that I should, little one, when you realize that this green smear is a beacon to light our way."

"What is it?" Zizi's big black eyes grew serious at Wise's tone.

"The way out; the exit; the solution of the mystery of the secret passage."

"Oh, Penny, tell me! You'll be the death of me if you keep the truth from me! I'm crazy with suspense!"

But Zizi's curiosity could not be gratified just then, for Fletcher came to say that Minna desired the girl's company.

Minna Varian had come to depend much on Zizi's charm and entertainment, and often sent for her when feeling especially blue or nervous.

Zizi had been waiting for an opportunity, and now as the nurse left her alone with Mrs. Varian, she gradually and deftly led the talk around to Betty as a baby.

"Tell me what you thought when you first saw your little daughter," Zizi said, in her pretty, coaxing way. "How old was she?"

"About an hour or so, I think," Minna said, reminiscently. "And my first thought was, 'Oh, thank God for a healthy, beautiful baby!' She was so lovely,—and so strong and perfect! I had hoped she would be all right, but I never looked for such a marvel as came to me!"

"And Mr. Varian was as pleased as you were!" Zizi said, gently.

"Oh, yes,—but," Minna's face clouded a little, "I don't know how to express it,—but he never seemed to love Betty as he did our first children. He admired her,— nobody could help it,—but he had a queer little air of restraint about her. It lasted all through life. I can't understand it,—unless he was jealous—"

"Jealous?"

"Yes, of my love and adoration of the child. Silly idea, I know, but I've racked my brain and I can't think of any other explanation."

"That doesn't explain the Varian pearls—"

"No; nothing can explain that! Oh, nothing explains anything! Zizi, you've no idea what I suffer! I wonder I keep my mind! Just think of a woman who never had to decide a question for herself, if she didn't want to,—who never had a care or responsibility that she didn't assume of her own accord,—who had a husband to care for her, a daughter to love her "

The poor woman broke down completely, and Zizi had her hands full to ward off the violent hysterics that attacked her at times.

Meantime, Pennington Wise, convinced of the origin of the green smear on Zizi's frock, was starting forth to prove his conviction.

Armed only with a powerful flashlight and a good sized hammer, he went out to the kitchen and through that to the cellar.

There, he went straight to the old well, and testing the rope as he did so, he let the bucket down as far as it would go. Then, with monkey like agility he began to clamber down,—partly supported by clinging to the rope, partly by getting firm footholds on the old stones that lined the well.

Scarcely had he started, when he experimentally drew his hand across the stones, and by his flashlight perceived a green smear, the counterpart of that on Zizi's frock. Also, the counterpart of that on Martha's hand.

Yet, the dead girl could scarcely have been in the well! So,—her assailant must have been.

However, he went on investigating.

He noted carefully the walls as he descended, and it was not until he almost reached the bottom of the dried up old well, that he noticed anything strange.

All of the wall was very rough and uneven but here was what appeared to be a distinct hole, roughly filled in with loose stones.

Standing now on the bottom of the well, slippery with moisture but no water above his shoe soles, he used his hammer to dislodge these stones, working carefully and slowly, but with a certainty of success.

"Fool that I was," he chattered to himself, "not to come down here the very first thing! To trust to Zizi was all right,—the kid couldn't notice this place, —but I had no business to trust that half baked sheriff or his man!"

His work soon disclosed the fact that the loose stones apparently closed the mouth of a deep hole.

When all that were loose had been either pulled out or pushed in, he found there was an aperture large enough to permit a man's body to pass through, and without hesitation, he scrambled through it.

His flashlight showed him that almost from the start the hole widened until it became a fair sized tunnel. Crawling along this for a hundred yards or so, he heard the splash of water, and soon he no longer needed his flashlight, as daylight streamed in through a narrow fissure in the rock.

It was fortunate for Wise that it did, for just ahead the tunnel descended sharply, and at the bottom, what was evidently the surf was surging in from the ocean.

It was quite dark below, and being unable to progress further, Wise backed out of the tunnel, it wasn't wide enough to turn around in, and reaching the well again, he ascended to the surface.

He went to his room, looked with satisfaction on the numerous smears of green and brown that disfigured his suit,—which he had taken care should be an old one.

No one knew what he had done, nor did any one know his destination when, half an hour later, he set off for the village.

He went to the inn and inquired where he could get the best motor boat that could be hired. A suitable one was found and its owner agreed to take Wise on an exploring expedition at the next low tide. This would not be until the following morning, so the detective went back to Headland House.

Then, he concentrated all his efforts and attention on the subject of the moving picture film that had been said to portray Betty Varian.

"Rod Granniss vows it was really Betty," Zizi insisted.

"He ought to know," said Wise. "A man in love with a girl doesn't mistake her identity. Besides, it's quite on the cards, Ziz. Say Betty is confined somewhere,—say she is let out for a little exercise in care of a jailer, of course,—say there's a M. P. contraption taking a picture of a crowd,—they often do,—pick up stray passers by you know, and say, Betty somehow got into the picture—"

"Oh, the jailer, as you call him, wouldn't let her!"

"More likely a woman in charge of her. And, maybe a woman not averse to taking the few dollars those people pay to actors who just make up a crowd. Well, say that happened, and then Betty, not daring to speak aloud, made her lips form the words 'I am Betty Varian,' in the hope that among a few thousands of lip readers in the country one might strike twelve!"

"Nobody could be so clever as all that, Pen!"

"She might be on a chance inspiration. Anyway, how else can you explain it?"

"Why, anybody might have said that, who wasn't Betty at all."

"But why? What would be the sense of it? and why would such a thing occur to anybody but Betty?"

"If it's true,—then you can find her! Surely you can track down a moving picture company!"

"Oh, it isn't that! It's tracking down the place where Betty is confined,—and—doing it while she is still alive. You see, Zizi, those ransom letters are true bills, and the villains have nearly reached the end of their patience."

"Then why don't you approve of Mrs. Varian's throwing the money over the cliff?"

"I may advise her to do it by Friday night,—if nothing happens in the meantime."

"But look here, Penny," Zizi said, after a thoughtful moment, "if your theory is the right one, why didn't Betty scream out, "I am Betty Varian!" and take a chance that somebody in the crowd would rescue her?"

"It would seem a natural thing to do, unless the girl had been so cowed by threats of punishment or even torture if she made any outcry when allowed to go for a walk. I'm visualizing that girl as kept in close confinement, but not in any want or discomfort. She is most likely treated well as to food, rooms and all that, but is not allowed to step out of doors except with a strict guard and under some terrible penalty if she attempts to make herself known. With Betty's love of fresh air and sunshine she would agree to almost anything to get out of doors. Then, too, if she merely formed those words without sound, the chance of their being read by a lip reader was really greater than the chance of doing any good by crying out aloud.

"Had she done that, whoever had her in charge would have whisked her away at once, and no one would have paid any attention to the slight disturbance."

"It's all perfectly logical and, oh, I hope Rodney gets some clue to the place where the picture was taken."

"I hope so, Ziz, but they've probably moved Betty away from there by now."

"Did you find out, Penny, what that stain on my frock was?"

"I did."

"Well?"

"Yes, my dear, you've struck it! You got that stain while you were down the well."

"Oh," Zizi's eyes lighted up; "of course I did! Those damp, mossy stones. And, then, oh, Wise one, just how did the same stain get on Martha's hand?"

"That, Zizi," Wise spoke almost solemnly, "is part of the solution of the whole great mystery."

CHAPTER 18: THE TRAP

IN a small but powerful motor boat Wise went on his voyage of exploration. The man who managed the craft was a stolid, silent person who obeyed Wise's orders without comment.

But when the detective directed that he go round the base of the headland, and skirt close to the rocks he grumbled at the danger.

"Be careful of the danger," Wise said, "steer clear of hidden reefs, but go close to the overhanging cliff, there where I'm pointing."

Skirting the cliff, at last Wise discovered what he was looking for, a small cave, worn in the rock by the sea. The floor of this cave rose sharply and it was with difficulty that Wise managed to scramble from the boat to a secure footing on the slippery wet rocks.

"Look out there," said the imperturbable boatman, "you'll get caught in there when the tide comes up. I never noticed that hole in the wall before, it must be out o' sight 'ceptin' at low tide."

"Stay where you are and wait for me," Wise directed, "if I'm not out here again in half an hour, go on home. But I'll probably be back in less than that."

"You will, if you're back at all! The tide will turn in fifteen minutes and in half an hour it'll be all you can do to get out!"

Disappearing, Wise began his climb up the floor of the cave, and at a point just above high water there was a fissure in the cliff which admitted air and some light. At this point the cave ran back for some distance, though still on a rising level. During the winter storms the ocean evidently had worn this tunnel in the rock.

Wise at once realized that this nature made tunnel ran on for some distance until it ended in the old well.

Using his flashlight when necessary, he made his way, until he reached the pile of stones which he himself had pushed out from the well and found to his satisfaction that he had indeed come to the well, and that his solution of the mystery of a secret passage into Headland House was accomplished.

But what a solution! The difficulty and danger of entrance or exit by means of that rock tunnel and that old well could scarce be exaggerated!

Moreover, all such entrances or exits must be made at the lowest ebb of the tide. But the cave was roomy, not uncomfortable, and the tunnel, though cramped in places, was fairly navigable.

There was plenty of room in the cave quite above reach of the highest tide, and the whole matter was clear and simple now that he saw it all, but he marveled at the energy and enterprise that could conceive, plan and carry out the various attacks.

Whoever the criminal, or the master criminal, might be, he had come up through that tunnel and well on the several occasions of the kidnapping of Betty, the murder of Martha, the abduction of North,—yes,—and Wise remembered the letter that had been mysteriously left on the hall table,—also the night the library had been entered,—clearly, the man came and went at will!

A master mind, Wise concluded, he had to deal with, and he set his own best energies to work on his problems.

The way between Headland House and the outer world was not easy of negotiation, but it was a way, and it was passable to a determined human being.

Wise was back inside the prescribed half hour, and the uninterested boatman took him back to the Harbor without question or comment as to his enterprise.

That afternoon, Wise called Minna and Doctor Varian into the library and closed the door.

Zizi was also present, her black eyes shining with anticipation, for she knew from Wise's manner and expression that he was making progress, and was about to disclose his discoveries.

"I have learned a great deal," the detective began, "but not all. At least, I have found the so called secret passage, which we all felt sure must exist."

He described the cave and the tunnel as he had found them, and the outlet into the old well, so carefully piled with loose stones that it would escape the observance of almost any searcher.

He told briefly but graphically of his exit from the well for a distance, and of his later entrance from the cave and his procedure to the well.

Zizi nodded her bird like little head, with an air of complete understanding, Doctor Varian was absorbedly interested and profoundly amazed, while Minna looked helplessly ignorant of just what Wise was talking about.

"I can't understand it," she said, piteously, "but never mind that, I don't care, if you say it's all so. Now, where is Betty?"

"That we don't know yet," Wise said, gently, "but we are on the way at last to find out. As I reconstruct the crime, now, that day that Betty returned for her camera, she must have done so under one of two conditions. Either her errand was genuine, in which case, she surprised the criminal here at some nefarious work,—or, which I think far more probable, she came back pretending it was for her camera, but really because of some message or communication which she had received purporting some good to her, but really a ruse of the criminal, who was here for the purpose of abducting the girl."

"For ransom?" asked Doctor Varian.

"Yes, for ransom. Now, he would naturally attack her in the hall. Perhaps she threw herself on the sofa, clung to it, and was carried off, still holding that yellow pillow, either unconsciously, or he may have used it to stifle her cries. There were two men involved, of that I am sure. For, when they had partly accomplished their purpose, Mr. Varian appeared at the door and one of the men had to intercept his entrance.

"I rather fancy the killing of Mr. Varian was unintentional,—or possibly, self defence, for these ruffians did not want to kill their blackmail victim. They may have parleyed with the father to pay them to release the girl, and when he showed fight, as he would, they did also, and as a result, Mr. Varian met his death.

"However, that is mere surmise. What we know is, that Betty was carried through the kitchen where the pillow fell,—still holding one of her hair pins, probably caught during the struggle,—and she was carried down the cellar stairs. During this trip her string of beads broke, and were scattered about. As we never found but a few, and those were under furniture or cupboards, I gather the villains picked up all they could see, lest they should be found as evidence."

"Which they were!" said Zizi.

"Which they were," Wise assented. "Then, they carried that girl whether conscious or chloroformed I can't say, down to the cellar, down the old well, through the tunnel to the cave. There they could wait any number of hours until the tide served, and take her away in a boat without attracting the notice of anybody."

"Most likely at night," Zizi put in.

"Most likely. Anyway, Mrs. Varian, that's my finding. It's all very dreadful, but horrifying as it is, it opens the way to better things. To go on, there can be no doubt that this same villain, and a clever one he is, returned here at night for plunder and on other errands.

"He came and left the letter found so mysteriously on the hall table. He came to rob the library safe, thinking the ransom money was in it. And he was spied upon and discovered by the maid, Martha, so that he ruthlessly strangled the poor thing to death, rather than face exposure."

"And then he abducted North!" Doctor Varian cried; "and it's easy to see why! North had doubtless also spied on him, and somehow he forced North to go away with him,—perhaps at pistol's point."

"Now our question is,—"

"Two questions!" Zizi cried; "first, who is the criminal,—and second where is he keeping Betty all this time?"

"Yes, and we know a great deal to start on." Wise spoke thoughtfully. "We know, almost to a certainty, that it is the man whom we call Stephen, because he wrote threatening letters signed 'Step.' We know he is diabolically clever, absolutely fearless, and willing to commit any crime or series of crimes to gain his end, which is merely the large sum of money he has demanded from Mrs. Varian, and which he had previously demanded from Mr. Varian, as blackmail."

"Why should he blackmail my husband?" Minna asked, tearfully, and Wise said, "There is not always a sound reason for blackmail, Mrs. Varian. Sometimes it is an unjust accusation or a mistaken suspicion. Any way, as you have often declared, Mr. Frederick Varian was a noble and upright man, and his integrity could not be questioned."

"Now, then," said Doctor Varian, "to find this master hand at crime. I am astounded at your revelations, Mr. Wise, and I confess myself utterly in the dark as to our next step."

"An animal that attacks in the open," Wise returned, "may be shot or snared. But a wicked, crafty animal may only be caught by a trap. I propose to set a trap to catch our foe. It is a wicked trap, but he is a wicked man. It will harm him physically, but he deserves to be harmed physically. It is a sly, underhand method, but so are his own. Therefore, I conclude that a trap is justified in his case."

"You mean a real, literal mantrap?" asked the doctor.

"I mean just that. I have already procured it and I propose to set it tonight. This is Thursday. As matters stand now, our 'Stephen' is assuming or at least hoping that Mrs. Varian means to accede to his last request and throw the money over the cliff tomorrow, Friday night. Now, I feel pretty positive that Stephen is not so confident of getting that money safely as he pretends he is. He must be more or less fearful of detection. I'm sure that he will return to this house tonight, by his usual mode of entrance, and will try to steal the money. Then he will disappear and he may or may not give up Betty."

"You think he'll come here? Tonight?" Doctor Varian was astonished.

"I do."

"Then we'll be ready for him! I fancy between us, Mr. Wise, we can account for him and his accomplice."

"Too dangerous, Doctor. He would kill us both before we knew it. "No, I'm going to set my trap. If he comes he deserves to be trapped. If he doesn't come, there is certainly no harm done."

"Where shall we hide the money?" asked Minna, nervously.

"It doesn't matter," and Wise's face set sternly. "He will never get as far as the money."

Hating his job, but fully alive to the justice and necessity of it, Wise set his trap that night. It was a real trap, and was set up in the kitchen in such a position that it faced the cellar door. It consisted of a short barreled shotgun which was mounted on an improvised gun carriage, made of a strong packing box.

This contrivance was fastened carefully to the kitchen wall about twelve feet in front of the cellar door, and when the door should be opened, the trap would be sprung and the shotgun discharged.

A steel spring fastened to the trigger, and a strong cord running to a pulley in the ceiling, thence to another, and finally to a pulley in the floor, and on to the door knob completed the deadly mechanism.

The tension of the spring was so carefully adjusted that an intruder might open the door a foot or more before the strain was carried to the trigger. This insured a sure aim and a clear shot.

Wise tested his trap thoroughly, and finally, with a grim nod of his head, declared it was all right. He had sent the servants and the women folks to bed, before beginning his work, and now he and Doctor Varian seated themselves in the library to await developments.

"As I said," Wise remarked, " 'Stephen' may not come at all, he may send an accomplice. Yet this I expect the most surely,—he will come himself."

"Have you no idea of his identity, Mr. Wise?" the doctor asked.

"Yes; I have an idea,—and if he does not come tonight, I will tell you who I think he is. But we will wait and see."

They waited, now silent and now indulging in a few low toned bits of conversation, when at two o'clock in the morning the report of the gun brought them to their feet and they raced to the kitchen.

The roaring detonation was still in their ears as they strode through the hall, and the smell of powder greeted them at the kitchen door.

The cellar door was open, and on the floor near it lay a man breathing with difficulty.

Doctor Varian dropped on his knees beside him, and his professional instinct was at once in full working order, even as his astonished voice exclaimed:

"Lawrence North!"

"As I expected," Wise said, "and well he deserves his fate. Will he live, Doctor?"

"Only a few moments," was the preoccupied reply. "I can do nothing for him. He received the full charge in the abdomen."

"Tell your story, North," Wise said, briefly; "don't waste time in useless groaning."

North glared at the detective.

"You fiend!" he gasped, gurgling in rage and agony.

"You're the fiend!" Varian said; "hush your vituperation and tell us where Betty is."

A smile of low cunning came over North's villainous face. He used his small remaining strength to say: "That you'll never know. You've spiked your own guns. Nobody knows but me,—and I won't tell!"

Alarmed, Wise tried another tone.

"This won't do, North," he said; "whatever your crime, you can't refuse that last act of expiation. Tell where she is, and die the better for it."

"No," gasped the dying man. "Bad I've lived and bad I'll die. You'll never find Betty Varian. There are standing orders to do away with her if anything happens to me, and,"—he tried to smile,—"something has happened!"

"It sure has," Wise said, and looked at him with real pity, for the man was suffering tortures. "But, I command you, North, by the blood you have shed, by the two human lives you have taken, by the heart of the wife and mother that you have broken,—I charge you, give up your secret while you have strength to do so!"

For a moment, North seemed to hesitate. A little stimulant administered by the doctor gave him a trifle more strength, but then his face changed,—he turned reminiscent.

"Good work," he said, it seemed, exultingly. "When I first found the cave a year ago, I began to plan how I could get the Varians to take this house. They little thought *I* brought it about through the real estate people—"

"Never mind all that," Wise urged him, "where's Betty?"

"Betty? ah, yes,—Betty " His mind seemed to wander again and Varian gave him a few drops more stimulant.

"Get it out of him," he said to the detective, "this will lose all efficacy in another few moments. He is going."

"Going, am I?" and North was momentarily alert. "All right, Doc, I'll go and my secret will go with me."

"Where is Betty?" Wise leaned over the miserable wretch, as if he would drag the secret from him by sheer will power.

But the other's will power matched his own.

"Betty," he said,—"oh, yes, Betty. Really, my wife's daughter, you know,—my step daughter,—I had a right to her, didn't I—"

"'Step'!" Wise cried, "Step, that you signed to those letters was short for Stepfather!"

"Yes, of course; my wife didn't mean to tell me that story,—didn't know she did,—she babbled in her sleep, and I got it out of her by various hints and allusions. Mrs. Varian never knew, so I bled the old man. My, he was in a blue funk whenever I attacked him about it!"

"Where is she now?" Wise hinted.

"No, sir, you don't get it out of me. You caught me,—damn you! now I'll make you wish you hadn't!" and Lawrence North died without another word.

Baffled, and spent with his exhausting efforts, Wise left the dead man in the doctor's care and returned to the library.

He found Zizi there. She had listened from the hall and had overheard much that went on, but she couldn't bring herself to go where the wounded man lay.

"Oh, Penny," she sobbed, "he didn't tell! Maybe if I had gone in I could have got it out of him! But I c couldn't look at him "

"Never mind, dear, that's all right. He wouldn't have told you, either. The man is the worst criminal I have ever known. He has no drop of humanity in his veins. As to remorse or regret, he never knew their meaning! Now, what shall we do? Is Mrs. Varian awake?"

"Yes; in mild hysterics. Fletcher is with her."

"Doctor Varian must go to her, and after that doubtless you can soothe her better than any one else. I'll get Potter and Dunn up here,—and I fervently hope it's for the last time!"

"Penny, your work was wonderful! You were right, a thing like that had to be trapped,—not caught openly. You're a wonder!"

"Yet it all failed, when I failed to learn where Betty is. I shall find her,—but I fear,—oh, Zizi, I fear that the evil that man has done will live after him,—and I fear for the fate of Betty Varian."

Zizi tried to cheer him, but her heart too was heavy with vague fears, and she left him to his routine work of calling the police and once again bringing them up to Headland House on a gruesome errand.

These things done, Wise went at once to North's bungalow in Headland Harbor. He had small hope of finding Joe Mills there, and as he had foreseen, that worthy had decamped. Nor did they ever see him again.

"I suppose," Wise said afterward, "he was in the cellar when North was killed; but I never thought of him then, nor could I have caught him as he doubtless fled away in the darkness to safety."

"Then it was a put up job, that scene of struggle and confusion in North's bedroom that day he disappeared?" Bill Dunn asked of Wise.

"Yes; I felt it was, but I couldn't see how he got away. You see, at that time, North began to feel that my suspicions were beginning to turn in his direction, and he thought by pretending to be abducted himself, he would argue a bold and wicked kidnapper again at work. At any rate, he wanted to get away, and stay away the better to carry on his dreadful purposes, and he chose that really clever way of departing. The touch of leaving his watch behind was truly artistic,—unless he forgot it. Well, now to find Betty Varian."

"Just a minute, Mr. Wise. How'd you come to think of looking for that cave arrangement"?

"After I began to suspect North, I watched him very closely. I had in my mind some sort of rock passage, and when I took him out in a boat, or Joe Mills, either, when we went close to that part of the rocks where the cave is, I noted their evident efforts not to look toward a certain spot. It was almost amusing to see how their eyes strayed that way, and were quickly averted. They almost told me just where to look!"

"Wonderful work!" Dunn exclaimed, heartily.

"No," Wise returned, "only a bit of psychology. Now to find Betty."

But though the detective doubtless would have recovered the missing girl, he had not the opportunity, for love had found a way.

By the hardest sort of work and with indefatigable perseverance, Granniss had gone from one to another of the various officials, mechanicians and even workmen of the moving picture company he was on the trail of and after maddening delays caused by their lack of method, their careless records and their uncertain memories, he finally found out where the picture of a crowd, in which Betty had appeared, was taken.

And then by further and unwearying search, he found an old but strongly built and well guarded house where he had reason to think Betty was imprisoned.

Finding this, he didn't wait for proofs of his belief, but telegraphed for Pennington Wise and Sheriff Potter to come there at once and gain entrance.

Rod's inexperience led him to adopt this course, but it proved a good one, for his telegram reached Wise the day after North's death, and he hurried off, Potter with him.

The house was in Vermont, and while Potter made the necessary arrangements with the local authorities, Wise went on to meet Granniss.

"There's the house," and Wise saw the rather pleasant looking old mansion. "I'm dead sure Betty's in there, but I can't get entrance, though I've tried every possible way."

But the arrival of the police soon effected an entrance, and armed with the knowledge of North's death as well as more material implements, they all went in.

Pretty Betty, as pretty as ever, though pale and thin from worry and fear, ran straight into Granniss' arms and nestled there in such absolute relief and content, that the other men present turned away from the scene with a choke in their throats.

If Granniss hadn't found her!

The news of North's death brought the jailers to terms at once. They were a man and wife, big, strong people, who were carrying out North's orders "to be kind and proper to the girl, but not to let her get away."

The moving picture incident had occurred just as Wise had surmised. On her daily walks for exercise, Betty was sometimes allowed to get into a crowd at the studio near by, and frequently she had tried her clever plan of silent talk. But only once had that plan succeeded.

Yet once was enough, and Granniss said, "Look here, you people, clear up all the red tape, won't you? Betty and I want to go home!"

"Run along," said Wise, kindly. "There's a train in an hour. Skip,—and God bless you!"

Their arrival at Headland House, heralded by a telegram to Zizi, had no unduly exciting effects on Minna Varian.

Doctor Varian watched her, but as he saw the radiant joy with which she clasped Betty in her arms, he had no fear of the shock of joy proving too much for her.

"Oh, Mother," Betty cried, "don't let's talk about it now. I'll tell you anything you want to know some other time. Now, just let me revel in being here!"

Nor did any one bother the poor child save to ask a few important questions.

These brought the information that Betty had been decoyed back to the house that day, by a false message purporting to be from Granniss, asking her to return after the rest left the house, and call him up on the telephone. This Betty tried to do, using her camera as an excuse.

But she never reached the telephone. Once in the house, she was grasped and the assailants, there were two, attempted to chloroform her. But chloroforming is not such a speedy matter as many believe and she was still struggling against the fumes when her father appeared.

North held Betty while the other man, who was Joe Mills, fought Frederick Varian, and, in the struggle, shot him.

This angered North so, that he lost his head. He almost killed Mills in his rage and fury, and seizing Betty, made for the secret passage.

On the way, her string of beads broke, the pillow which they used to help make her unconscious was dropped on the kitchen floor, and then she was carried down the well, through the tunnel and cave and away in a swift motor boat.

But in a half conscious state, all these things were like a dream to her.

"A dream which must not be recalled," said Granniss, with an air of authority that sat well upon him.

"My blessing," Minna said, fondling the girl. "Never mind about anything, now that I have you back. I miss your father more than words can say, but with you restored, I can know happiness again. Let us both try to forget

Later, a council was held as to whether to tell Minna the true story of Betty's birth.

The two young people had to be told, and Doctor Varian was appealed to for a decision regarding Minna.

"I don't know," he said, uncertainly. "You see it explains the pearls,—"

"I'll tell you," Granniss said. "Don't let's tell Mother Varian now. Betty and I will be married very soon, and after that we can see about it. Or, if she has to know at the time of the wedding, we'll tell her then. But let her rejoice in her new found child as her own child as long as she can. Surely she deserves it."

"And *you* don't care?" Betty asked, looking at him, wistfully.

"My darling! I don't care whether you're the daughter of a princess or pauperess,—you'll soon be my wife, and Granniss is all the name you'll ever want or need!"

"Bless your sweet hearts," said Zizi, her black eyes showing a tender gleam for the girl she had so long known of, and only now known.

"And bless your sweetheart, when you choose one!" Betty said, her happy heart so full of joy that her old gayety already began to return.

THE END

Other Resurrected Press Mysteries From Carolyn Wells

Resurrected Press Mysteries From Louis Tracy

The Albert Gate Mystery
Four men murdered and a fortune in diamonds belonging to the Turkish Sultan stolen, while the Foreign Office official in charge has gone missing. Was it a common jewelry theft or was it a case of international intrigue? This is the question that barrister detective Reginald Brett must solve.

The Bartlett Mystery
When Ronald Tower is murdered on his way to a bridge game on the yacht Sans Souci it at first appears a common crime. But as Rex Carshaw finds, a tragic case of mistaken identity leads to political scandal among the rich and powerful of New York.

The Strange Case of Mortimer Fenley
When the wealthy Mortimer Fenley is struck down by a shot from an express rifle on the steps of his mansion, detectives Winter and Furneaux of Scotland Yard must find the culprit. Was it the artist who claimed he was painting a picture at the time of the shot? The disaffected younger son? Or is there another suspect?

The Stowmarket Mystery
For five generations the Fergus-Hume family has been cursed. Each of the baronets has met a violent end. When the fifth baronet is found slain by a ceremonial Japanese dagger, suspicion falls on his cousin David. It falls to barrister detective Reginald Brett to prove his innocence and find the real murder in a case that spans two continents and as many centuries.

Visit www.resurrectedpress.com

Resurrected Press Mysteries by J. S. Fletcher

The Orange-Yellow Diamond
When an elderly pawnbroker is murdered in the London parish of Paddington, a young, down on his luck writer is accused of the crime. But then it's found the pawnbroker had had in his possession an extraordinary South African diamond worth over eighty-thousand pounds — a diamond that's now missing. It falls to Melky Rubenstein to unravel the mystery and prove the young man's innocence.

The Middle Temple Murder
When an elderly man's body is found on the steps of chambers in the Midde Temple, one of the Inns of Court, it falls to newspaperman Frank Spargo and Detective-Sergeant Rathbury to solve the crime. The murdered man, for indeed it was murder, was found with no money or identification on his person except for a piece of paper with the name and address of a young barrister. Who is the victim? Why was he killed? Who is the murderer?

Scarhaven Keep
Bassett Oliver, the famed actor, has gone missing. When Oliver fails to show for a rehearsal, aspiring playwright Richard Copplestone finds himself sent to the small village of Scarhaven on the northern coast of England to track down the actors movements. What he finds is mystery. Find the answers as Copplestone unravels the mystery of Scarhaven Keep.

Visit www.resurrectedpress.com

Resurrected Press Mysteries by Fergus Hume

The Green Mummy
Professor Braddock hoped to compare the burial practices of the Egyptians with those of the ancient Peruvians with his latest acquisition, the mummy of the last Inca, Caxas. But on arrival, the packing case proved to hold not the mummy, but the body of his assistant Sidney Bolton. It falls to Archie Hope to discover the murderer if he is to marry the professors step-daughter, Lucy Kendal. Who killed Bolton and where is the mummy? Was it the sea captain Hervey? The mysterious Don Pedro? Cockatoo the Polynesian servant? The professor, himself? And what has become of the emeralds? These are the questions that Hope must answer amongst the secrets of the past in The Green Mummy.

The Mystery of a Hansom Cab
"Truth is said to be stranger than fiction, and certainly the extraordinary murder which took place in Melbourne Friday morning goes a long way towards verifying that saying." Thus opens The Mystery of a Hansom Cab, the best selling mystery of the nineteenth century. When a man is found dead in a hansom cab one of Melbourne's leading citizens is accused of the murder. He pleads his innocence, yet refuses to give an alibi. It falls to a determined lawyer and an intrepid detective to find the truth, revealing long kept secrets along the way. Fergus Hume's first and perhaps most famous mystery... The Mystery Of A Hansom Cab.

Visit www.resurrectedpress.com

Resurrected Press Mysteries from the Dr. John Thorndyke Series

Dr. John Thorndyke - Lecturer on Medical Jurisprudence and Forensic Medicine. Before Bones, before CSI, before Quincy, M.E– there was Dr. John Thorndyke solving the most baffling cases of Edwardian London using the latest tools of medical science. Read about his cases in:

The Eye of Osiris
John Bellingham, noted Egyptologist has vanished not once but twice in the same day. Now Dr, Thorndyke must unravel the tangled claims on his estate, solve the riddle of the missing man and find the "Eye of Osiris".

The Mystery of 31 New Inn
When Dr. Jervis is whisked away in a coach with no windows to an unknown location to treat a man in a coma from undivulged causes it is Dr. Thorndyke who must come up with the solution.

The Red Thumb Mark
The first of Dr. Thorndyke's cases finds him trying to prove the innocence of a young man accused of being a diamond thief despite the fact that his finger print was found at the scene of the crime.

John Thorndyke's Cases
More cases of medical mysteries as told by his trusted assistant Jervis, M.D. Eight stories of crime and deduction in Edwardian London.

Visit www.resurrectedpress.com

Resurrected Press Mysteries by John R. Watson & Arthur J. Rees

The Hampstead Mystery

High Court Justice Sir Horace Fewbanks found shot dead in his Hampstead home, a butler with a criminal past, a scorned lover and a hint of scandal. These are the elements of the Hampstead Mystery that Detective Inspector Chippenfield of Scotland Yard must unravel with the assistance of the ambitious Detective Rolfe. But will he be able to sort out the tangled threads of this case and arrest the culprit before he is upstaged by the celebrated gentleman detective Crewe. Follow the details of this amazing case at it plays out across Hampstead, London and Scotland until it reaches a stunning conclusion in the courts of the Old Bailey.

The Mystery of the Downs

When Harry Marsland was caught in a sudden down pour he sought shelter at Cliff Farm. Met at the door by a young woman clearly expecting someone else he is only too glad to get inside to wait out the storm. When they hear a noise upstairs in the deserted house they investigate only to discover the body of the farm's owner, Frank Lumsden, dead of a gunshot wound. Who then, killed Lumsden, and why? Who was the woman expecting and did she have any roll in the murder? These are the questions that private detective Crewe must answer in The Mystery of the Downs.

Visit www.resurrectedpress.com

Other Resurrected Press Mysteries

Mysteries on a Train

Before the Orient Express there was:

The Rome Express by Arthur Griffiths
A man is found dead in his first class sleeping compartment on the express from Rome to Paris. Who was his murderer? The Countess? The English General? His brother the clergy man? The maid who has disappeared? Is the French justice system up to solving the crime? Read about it in The Rome Express.

The Passenger from Calais by Arthur Griffiths
Colonel Basil Annesley finds he is the only passenger on the train from Calais to Lucerne. That is until a mysterious woman shows up at the last minute to book a compartment. Who is after her? What is her secret? Is she a criminal or a victim? Read about it in The Passenger from Calais

Visit us at www.resurrectedpress.com

About Resurrected Press

A division of Intrepid Ink, LLC, Resurrected Press is dedicated to bringing high quality, vintage books back into publication. See our entire catalogue and find out more at www.ResurrectedPress.com.

About Intrepid Ink, LLC

Intrepid Ink, LLC provides full publishing services to authors of fiction and non-fiction books, eBooks and websites. From editing to formatting, from publishing to marketing, Intrepid Ink gets your creative works into the hands of the people who want to read them. Find out more at www.IntrepidInk.com.

CPSIA information can be obtained at www.ICGtesting.com
Printed in the USA
BVOW06s2238100116

432452BV00018B/70/P